About the Author

Graeme Smith is a Fourth Degree Black Belt and has practiced Kenpo Karate for 30 years. The catalyst for writing this book has been the many finds he has made from the Bronze Age whilst metal detecting. He also has a collection of over 400 knapped flints which he has found whilst field walking. The majority of these flints date from the late Neolithic to the early Bronze Age periods.

I dedicate this book to my two beautiful grandchildren
Mia and Leo, two treasured gifts in life.

Graeme Richard Smith

AGRAR OF THE CORNISH

AUSTIN MACAULEY
PUBLISHERS LTD.

A CIP catalogue record for this title is available from the British Library.

ISBN 9781786294562 (Paperback)
ISBN 9781786294579 (Hardback)
ISBN 9781786294586 (E-Book)
www.austinmacauley.com

First Published (2016)
Austin Macauley Publishers Ltd.
25 Canada Square
Canary Wharf
London
E14 5LQ

ACKNOWLEDGMENTS

My grateful thanks to the many Landowners who have kindly given me permission over the years to metal detect and field walk on their land – Messrs J M Kennaway, C Gibbins, B Brown,
J Strawbridge, K Banks, A Vinnicombe, Mr Pratt and Dave.
Thanks also to fellow detectorists John Sturley, Bernie & Rose Abbott, Alan Townsend and Graham Staddon who have accompanied me many times to discover Britain's hidden past and to Troy and Nexus my two constant companions who have helped me to discover Bronze Age Britain.
Also to Jennie Holvey for her enchanting poem entitled 'This Ancient Land' which was specially written by her for Agrar of the Cornish.

This Ancient Land
by Jennie Holvey

Oh people of Cornwall with tin in your blood
Your ancestors speak, listen and look

Their voices are heard in the wind as it blows
In the rain as it freezes and turns to snow

Warm summer breeze and the cold winter gale
Stirs the ghosts to tell their tale

Of secrets and myths from times of old
Of precious gifts of tin and gold

The waves roll in and break on the shore
Bringing messages from those who have lived before

Glittering water in streams flowing fast
Shaped by the lives of those who have passed

Wisdom embedded in the stones on the moor
Ancient knowledge within is stored

Mysteries unveiled as the mists and fog clear
The spirits of those whom the Gods held dear

Many have walked this ancient land
Their footprints left in the earth and sand

So open your hearts, your soul, your mind
The Gods' gifts are there for you to find

Prologue

Britain 8000 BC

As the ice melted and the seas started to rise, the Tin God Cassitar looked down and could see that soon many islands would form. He had great wealth in the way of metal and needed a safe place to store the large tin deposits he had accumulated. Soon two large islands formed as the sea swallowed up the land that surrounded them. Cassitar looked down at the larger island and saw its future in worldly affairs; he knew that the inhabitants would one day virtually rule the world by having a mighty empire. He felt a great love for the area which lay at the far south west of this island.

The metal of the Gods is bronze and is made from copper and tin so, as a gift to this land's future people, Cassitar decided to hide his tin beneath the ground there. The God knew that copper would also be found close by and so the deed was done.

Just as the sea decided to claim no more land and the final shape of this island formed around 10,000 years ago, the God buried his tin in a land that is now called Cornwall.

Afterwards he looked down from above and smiled, for he knew it was safe and ready for a time when man would discover and use it to make bronze for themselves and for peoples from faraway lands.

Cassitar still looks down from time to time on his beloved people, the Cornish, who even to this day have a tiny amount of his tin in their blood.

CHAPTER 1

South West Cornwall, 1000BC

"Who are they Father?" asked the boy.

"Greeks, I think," came the reply.

"How do you know that?"

"They have visited these shores many times before, my son."

"Should we go back to the village and tell the others or shall we go down to the beach and welcome them to our land, Father?"

"We must firstly observe them and see if they come with swords to steal our tin or if they come with goods to trade with us."

"Where do they come from?"

"It is said they live in a land far away, across the seas, and that they live in strange houses that we could not even imagine, where the sun provides them with more warmth than it gives to this island."

Father and son lay side by side upon the cliffs overlooking the shore and observed the boat as it came in close enough for several of the Greek crew to slide down into the seawater that separated this island from Europe many millennia ago. As the men swam to the shore the Greek ship backed away to deeper waters and waited.

The sky was blue; its reflection lay in the clear still waters of the bay. The golden sand lay like a majestic carpet which followed the shoreline for miles in both directions. The countless billions of grains of sand were controlled by wind and tide, which were constantly shaping them at their will.

Father and son eagerly observed the men on the beach as they appeared to have carried with them items which they now were laying out and displaying upon the golden sand.

***

The father's name was Agrar, his son was called Agrin. Their tribal ancestors had crossed over the waters two centuries before and settled here in ancient Cornwall 3200 years ago. Their village lay half a mile away from where they were now observing the unexpected visitors from the eastern Mediterranean.

"What are they doing, Father?" asked a curious Agrin.

"I think they are offering us gifts or displaying objects for us to trade with them," answered Agrar.

The Greeks had indeed laid out many items on the sand which they had brought ashore on a small craft which they had towed behind them whilst swimming ashore. The Greeks appeared to have no weapons upon them which came as a big relief to Agrar as he remembered the last visit by men such as these who came bearing arms in many ships, forcing Agrar and his people to give them tin without any way of payment. That was six years ago when Agrin was aged two, but to Agrar it seemed like yesterday. That was when Agrar's wife Alvaria was taken away by the last visitors from the Mediterranean to come here.

"Go to the village, Agrin, and tell our people to gather their spears, bows and arrows. Tell them to make their way here as soon as they can."

"Yes, Father," replied Agrin, who then sneaked away and, once safely out of site from where he and his father had been, ran back to the village as fast as his legs could carry him.

Meanwhile, Agrar continued to watch the visitors who had now finished displaying their goods upon the sand and had walked back into the cool calm waters where they stood in a row facing the beach. Each man was stood up straight with the sea lapping up to his knees and after a while, Agrar decided to stand up and show himself to the Greeks. He was far enough away from them to feel no immediate danger to himself. His hair was as dark as night and his skin was the colour of the light brown soil of the fields from this part of Cornwall. He was tall and slim, clean shaven and had the strength of a bear, the courage of a lion and the wisdom of a king. Agrar had been specially trained in beach warfare. This involved learning to fight and run on the soft sand of the beaches found locally. He could outrun any man, woman or child on the sand so unless these Greeks were trained likewise, they were no match for Agrar. He slowly made his way down to the beach, leaving his spear behind. No fear was in his mind but he would remain very cautious and be on guard at all times.

The midday sun was high above him and the summer heat shimmered upon the sand, creating a haze between Agrar and the Greeks.

He approached the matting upon the shoreline to see what goods lay on the sand. As he approached, the four Greeks watched impassively as Agrar walked along inspecting the objects before him. He showed no emotion whilst doing so but inside was marvelling at the Greeks' trade goods. These included the latest weapons crafted by the Greeks whose technology in metallurgy was way in advance of the ancient tribes of Devon and Cornwall, where copper and more importantly tin was available. There were weapons and tools made of the very highly revered and sacred metal of bronze, which was a gift of discovery to man sanctioned by the Gods.

Next to the bronze items lay beautiful and highly decorated ceramics, gold wrist and armbands, textiles and lastly amphoras filled with wine.

***

Agrin had now reached the village which consisted of fifty roundhouses. Soon smoke signals were being sent up into the skies, alerting nearby villages and houses of possible danger.

The ancient peoples from this part of Cornwall had prepared for such a time as this after the last unwelcome visitors from lands afar had been and gone, leaving a bitter taste in the mouths of this community who traded with their tin.

Men and women now gathered arms together with any child aged ten or over. They would make their way to strategic points along the coast and wait. Each person carried a horn to blow and all knew the signals to listen and respond to, Agrin was aged only eight and so would have to remain behind at the village.

CHAPTER 2

Agrar stepped a few paces back from the matting and looked the Greeks in the eyes who responded by giving their attention to him as the sea gently lapped against their legs. Agrar nodded his head in approval to which the Greeks responded likewise.

The men waded out of the water and walked up onto the shore. One of them produced a brightly coloured cloth. He turned seaward and waved it above his head. This was a signal to the waiting ship and moments later a pair of homing birds were released into the air. Up and away into the distance they flew, the feathers of their wings now feeling the freedom of flight for which they were designed by Mother Nature. The birds would fly above sea until a fleet of thirty heavier and slower Greek ships were sighted by them. Here they would land aboard the craft which would transport the tin back to where they had set sail from many weeks before.

The Greeks were desperate for tin to harden their copper into bronze. They possessed all the copper they could ever need but their enemies now had control of all the tin in the eastern Mediterranean. Weapons could, of course, be made from just copper but any army would have a most definite advantage if their weapons had been hardened with tin. These travellers from afar had come desperately seeking the precious tin and now the people of

Bronze Age Cornwall would trade in an era that thrived in this ancient time during early European metallurgy.

***

The homing birds flew high and far in search of the bigger Greek ships, following several days behind the smaller scouting ship which now lay anchored in Cornish waters in front of Agrar who now stood awaiting the next move from the Greeks.

Back at the village, Agrin, son of Agrar, was excitedly telling the other children all about what he and his father had seen. He was a good storyteller, just like his mother had been. Agrin had no memories of her, a fact that was deeply felt by him, occasionally causing him great sadness. Now people from the surrounding area were gathering and making their way to the coastline in response to the alarm.

***

Three of the Greeks now sat down upon the fine golden sand. The fourth, a man about the same height as Agrar, slowly approached him. The two men stood squarely facing one another, the Greek speaking first.

"My name is Pyris," he said, together with an outstretched arm.

Agrar cautiously looked him up and down before eventually responding likewise and shaking his hand. *How is it this Greek speaks in our tongue?* he thought to himself. He tried to make conversation with Pyris but the Greek had a vocabulary of only about sixty words.

Pyris communicated with Agrar using these words but also pointed, nodded and made gestures which were universally understood by others.

Agrar relaxed a little as he observed the Greeks and felt that peaceful trade would this time take place between them.

They desperately needed tin and an armada was coming to get it. Pyris picked up a stick laying close by and together with his three fellow Greeks drew upon the wet sand near the water's edge of the now receding tide. Soon a large pictorial explanation lay in front of Agrar showing him how many ships would come in a few days and also how much tin was needed by the Greeks. Pyris handed the stick to Agrar who showed him what he and his people would want in return from the Greeks. It didn't take long for the two men to agree on a trading deal.

***

The coastline was now ready for any occurrence that could happen, as a hundred armed men and women now lay in wait for Agrar's signal should it be needed.

Amongst these defenders of ancient Cornwall was the Dog Warrior, who had under his control a pack of twenty specially trained dogs, obedient to his every command. They too waited for Agrar's signal.

***

At the village, Agrin was wondering what was happening at the beach, so much so that his curiosity took control of him and he sneaked away out from the village to find out for himself. Whilst he did so, his father Agrar was now showing Pyris, by drawing pictures in the sand, that his people would erect timber jetties out from the beach to accommodate the ships that would soon come and be loaded with tin.

The men shook hands once more and Pyris together with the other Greeks swam back to their ship.

Agrar turned and walked back up to where he had left his spear. He climbed up to the highest point along the cliffs and blew his horn to signal all those awaiting. The people of his tribe soon came and gathered around him and once all had assembled they sat around their leader to listen to the news about the larger ships on their way to Cornwall. Everyone was now given instructions to go and gather the timbers required to build the moorings for the approaching Greek fleet.

Agrar and his people had a large stockpile of logs and timber at their disposal which would make this an easier task than not.

Everyone soon understood what they each had to do and just as they were all dispersing, along came Agrin who tentatively approached his father.

"Agrin, you should not leave the village until you are told to do so."

"Sorry, Father, but I had a strange feeling."

"What do you mean, my son?"

"It was as if someone was calling for me to come here." There was a reason for this.

Agrar gave out a big belly laugh in response to this and said to Agrin, "Son, you have been out in the sun and heat for too long today, come here and climb up onto my shoulders and I will carry you back to the village and you can imagine you are a giant."

Agrin liked this idea and was soon imagining all sorts as he and his father made their way back home to the village. He imagined himself as a mighty warrior as he travelled through the air supported by his father's strong shoulders. He looked up at the clear blue sky and asked his father about the Greeks.

"Father, do they have birds of the sea, where they come from?"

"Who, Agrin?"

"The Greeks, Father."

"I do not know, my son."

"I think birds are the luckiest creatures of all."

"How is that so, my son?"

"Well," said Agrin as he watched the gulls soaring high above them. "These birds can fly, they can walk and they can swim on the sea that surrounds us, so father, surely they are blessed by all of the Gods. Do you believe what they say about these creatures, Father?"

"What do you mean, Agrin?"

"That the gulls are messengers for the Sky God and they were given the gift of flight so they can fly high up into the heavens to tell him of things that happen to the Earth Goddess on which we now stand."

Agrar looked up at the gulls in flight and said, "It is what our ancestors have told us, my son, and so it is my belief also."

CHAPTER 3

The samples of trade goods from the beach had now been taken back to the village by Agrar's tribe. This night was one for celebration and in the preceding days everyone for miles around would help construct the mooring jetties for the Greek ships to tie up to.

That night the camp fire crackled and spat as the wild boar slowly roasted above it until the meat was ready to devour ravenously.

Agrar and his men sampled some wine from the distant home of the Greek sailors. The village women sat examining finely decorated textiles that had been woven in warmer climates.

Agrin and the other children were making fierce scary shapes in the form of shadows from the light of the roaring fire.

In the bay, the Greek ship lay resting in the calm Cornish waters.

A woman's silhouette could be seen from the shore looking up at the moon. She was a mystery to the Greeks as she had lost her memory years before after she had been beaten for trying to escape from her captors who were the enemies of Pyris and his fellow countrymen. One day after a mighty battle she was rescued by the Greeks and taken care of. She had taught Pyris the tongue of the Cornish and also she knew about tin, but to all other things they

remained a forgotten memory until today. This day as she had watched the men on the beach trading with one another a familiarity was felt by her as she looked upon the landscape and its people.

The moon was full and bright this night as she gazed upon it.

Agrar was also gazing up at the moon and as he did so the hairs on the back of his neck stood up and he felt something strange at that moment but could not explain what or why to himself.

That night Agrar had many strange dreams, including one of his lost wife Alvaria calling out to him to come and rescue her. In the dream she wore a white gown made from very fine thread and woven into a style that was not familiar to him. Her hair and skin colour had changed slightly but because of the emotion of the dream, Agrar knew it was her and not another woman similar to Alvaria. His dream spirit had travelled the universe most nights as he lay asleep searching for the woman he loved and now this very night a connection had been made with her. Another dream came after this one, a powerful and unpleasant dream. It was of Agrin being taken by the sea until he was dead. In this dream Agrar could do nothing to save his son and now as he slept, turmoil and strife ran amok inside his sleeping mind. His dream spirit was drawn back to his body by all the emotion and now the mighty chieftain awoke into a state of confusion and fear. He sat up, his hands covering his face as he tried to work out what his dreams were telling him. Agrar thought long and hard, deciding half-heartedly to blame the dream on the Greek wine of which he had drunk much that evening. He still felt spooked as he tried to settle himself once more to sleep which he eventually did.

As Agrar's people slept that night the Greek fleet were nearing Cornwall, where their last desperate hope of obtaining tin could happen.

***

"Wake up, Father," said Agrin as the mighty chieftain slowly responded to his son's request. Agrin was in a squat position observing his father as he awoke. Their eyes met in the dimly lit roundhouse just as the morning sun rays radiated into it. Agrar briefly remembered the disturbing dream about his son and then in an instant dismissed it as if it were nothing. Agrar held out his arms towards his son.

"Come here, boy," he commanded. He embraced Agrin and as he did so, felt the luckiest man alive to have such a son. As the two embraced they could both feel the beat of each other's hearts through their chests which were both bare and pressed hard together.

"Son, I love you so very much."

"And I love you, Father," came the reply.

Agrar released his embrace and marvelled at Agrin's face, his eyes and nose reminding him of his long lost wife Alvaria.

The boy smiled and snuggled into Agrar's left side as they both gazed out of the doorway to witness the sunrise.

"What will happen today, Father?" asked Agrin.

"Today, my son, I will start to organise all the people from this village and surrounding area into work parties."

"Can I help, Father?"

"Yes, but you must wait until tomorrow."

Agrin's face showed slight disappointment which Agrar immediately remedied by saying "Son, I need you to sharpen my spear tips and my sword. I entrust this task to you, Agrin, as one day you will be chieftain and must show that you are a man at one with his weapons."

"But, Father…"

"No buts, Agrin, just do as I say."

Agrin knew he must obey and so just rolled his eyes.

"Let us go and see if there is any meat left on that big fat boar they roasted last night."

Agrin laughed and followed his father out into the morning air. They both walked over to the fire and examined the boar.

"Here, son, take your knife and cut enough meat to last you and I the rest of the day. Then we will eat early and have as full a day as possible."

Agrar and Agrin sat close together next to the now smouldering fire and as they ate the village slowly came to life with people emerging from the roundhouses of the village.

"Father," said Agrin.

"Yes, my son, what is it?"

"Last night I dreamt of a woman calling to me."

"Who was she?" asked Agrar.

"I don't know."

Agrin started to describe the woman he had seen in his dream. As he did so, Agrar remembered his dreams and as he listened to Agrin's description he knew and felt that it was Alvaria who was being described to him.

Agrin had often asked his father about his mother and had an idea of what she looked like, but now Agrin's description far exceeded anything ever told to him before by his father.

"Come, Agrin, we must go over to the river valley and seek out the Teller of Dreams."

"But why, Father?"

"Because you have just described more about your mother than has ever been told to you before."

This excited the young boy's mind and soon father and son set off over the hill to the west and down into the valley to find the Teller of Dreams. But now Agrar was troubled, as he remembered the terror of the sea claiming the life of Agrin in his dreams.

CHAPTER 4

In the valley of Lupax lived Mendax, Teller of Dreams.

No one knew how old he was, but he had lived in the lifetime of Agrar's father and grandfather and it was said that the Death God had forgotten of his existence and so he would live forever and never die.

Mendax had the ability to see beyond the physical world and now the mighty chieftain Agrar together with his son Agrin approached his roundhouse. As they both came over the hill a group of ten deer scattered away and into some woods.

The smoke from the roundhouse rose vertically without the disturbance of wind or rain. The morning mist clung to the hillside as the two figures breathed in the freshness of a new day.

"Father, what is the Teller of Dreams called?"

"He is known as Mendax, but do not fear his strangeness, my son."

The boy reached out and held his father's hand as they both descended into the valley of Lupax.

As they got nearer and nearer to the mystic's house the mist suddenly totally cleared and a figure emerged from within the house. There stood Mendax; he glanced at the two approaching figures and sat down on a bench that surrounded most of the Bronze Age roundhouse. His hair was grey and most of his face was covered by a well-groomed beard and moustache. His stature was slight as he lived on nuts, berries and fruit.

The two visitors walked over to where he sat and stood, respectfully awaiting a response.

Mendax lifted his head up to look Agrar in the eye. "Ah, the mighty chieftain Agrar and his son, to what do I owe this visit to my humble home?"

"I seek out your knowledge and wisdom, Mendax."

"In which way is this, Agrar?"

"In the way of dreams, both those of Agrin and myself."

Agrar described the dream of Alvaria to Mendax who replied by saying, "Come over to the stream and we shall see if the waters will reveal to us your answers."

Agrar and Agrin followed the Teller of Dreams to a large pool of water set on a bend in the stream.

Mendax took out his knife and said, "I must have twenty hairs from each of your heads."

Agrar nodded and bowed down so that Mendax could cut his hair first.

The Teller of Dreams reached over to Agrin to cut his hair. "Do not be afraid, boy," said Mendax with a look in his eye that instantly made Agrin feel at ease.

The hairs were mixed together in the hands of Mendax as both father and son watched in anticipation.

"Be quiet and still now," said Mendax as he knelt down and sprinkled the hairs upon the pool of still water. He uttered a few works in a tongue not known to Agar and the three watched and waited for the waters to answer.

Agrin's hair was much softer and finer than his father's and as the boy looked on, his now floating hairs started to turn silver in colour. The boy looked on in fascination now but was also a little fearful of all these strange events.

After a few moments Agrar's cut hairs started to turn gold in colour and formed two circles upon the water. No sooner has this happened, the silver hairs from Agrin started to form one large circle around the two gold circles of hair.

Mendax leant over to a large nearby rock and picked it up. He chanted a few more words before throwing the rock onto the floating circles of hair. There was no splash as the rock hit the water, to which father and son took a step back in surprise as Mendax crouched down and looked deeply into the water.

After a few minutes he stood up to face Agrar and spoke. "Yours and your son's dreams of your wife can be answered by you going to the Greek ship that is now anchored in the bay."

"But what did you see?" asked Agrar.

"The waters showed me the ship and no more, all will be answered there."

Agrar did not quite understand this, but decided that he must go soon with men and board the Greek ship.

Agrar instructed Agrin to walk over to the roundhouse and wait for him as he had some other business to discuss with Mendax. The boy slowly walked away and as he did so his father turned to Mendax and told him of his other dream of his son being claimed by the sea.

"Agrar, you must bleed your arm into the water now, to get your answer."

Mendax cut into Agrar's outstretched arm with his knife until the blood constantly dripped into the water.

"Shut your eyes now, Agrar," commanded Mendax as he looked once more into the water, this time using a stick to produce a whirlpool within it.

"What of my son?" demanded Agrar.

Silence ensued and then Mendax let out a gasp of despair.

"Tell me, what of my son?" demanded Agrar again as he opened his eyes.

Mendax bowed to the mighty chieftain and prepared nervously to answer him.

"The sea will claim the life of your son, Agrar."

"NO, you are wrong old man, not my son, no!"

"Then maybe the Gods will change what I have seen."

"If this is any doing of the Gods then curse them!" shouted Agrar. "It's those Greeks, they have brought all this upon us."

Mendax made sure he was not going to say any more to upset Agrar. "Come, let us return to my home and your son."

The two men walked over to where Agrin was waiting.

"Come, my son, we must return to the village and select warriors to go with me to the Greek ship."

"But why warriors, Father?"

"Because those Greeks have somehow brought a curse upon us with them."

Father and son set off up over the hill which looked down upon the valley of Lupax, watched by Mendax who was now wishing this day had never happened as he knew that Agrar, the mighty Cornish chieftain, was now angry and full of rage. He would show the Greeks no mercy should they not give him an answer or explanation that was pleasing to him or that could put his now tortured mind at ease.

CHAPTER 5

During the Bronze Age, water was revered by the peoples of this time. Water was sacred here and all over Europe as it held the secrets to life, past, present and future; gifts and offerings of bronze and gold objects were placed into water and left forever – it was the most powerful, spiritual and supernatural substance known to our Bronze Age ancestors all those millennia ago. Water could not lie and now the soothsayer Mendax had told Agrar of what was to come.

***

As Agrar reached the top of the hill overlooking his village he blew a warning signal upon his horn that he and his people knew was an alarm and was heard from miles around. Now the warrior class of these peaceful people gathered weapons and awaited the chieftain's return to their village.

"Son, when we reach home I want you to stay inside the house and, as I instructed you yesterday, to sharpen my weapons and tools. Check on the shafts of my spearheads and on the arrows in my store. Make sure they are true and that they will fly to where my bow aims them. Do you understand, my son?"

"Yes, Father," answered Agrin as he looked upon his father's heavy frown and worried face.

Agrar walked with a heavy step in his stride and his mind began to think irrationally which was very unusual for a man like him.

Agrin went straight into the roundhouse and, as he did so, took a final look at his father before disappearing through the doorway.

"What is wrong, Agrar?" asked an old woman as he once more blew upon his horn sending a signal go all around that he was now ready.

Men soon began to arrive at the village including the Dog Warrior, to whom Agrar spoke first. "Man of Dogs, you must come with me and bring your dogs out into the sea to surround the Greek ship which has come to curse our land."

"Curse? What curse do you tell of?"

"Just do as I say for now and I will explain everything to you later." Agrar selected three trusted Men of Arms to go with him and the Dog Warrior to the beach. "Agrin!" shouted the chieftain, "Bring me out my fighting spear and dagger."

Shortly after, Agrin emerged from the roundhouse with the two weapons his father had requested.

Agrar told all those who had gathered that he had to now go and make sure the Greeks were true to their word and not there to curse the village or cause unrest.

"You stay here, my son," said Agrar, whilst running his fingers through the boy's hair and looking at him with the true love of a father. Agrar blew his horn once more as he and the men he had selected made their way towards the beach.

***

Agrar's ancestors had come to Cornwall many generations beforehand and were originally from Southern

Spain. These ancestors had brought a special breed of dog with them which had adapted itself to water and now the Dog Warrior had at his command twenty of these dogs which would swim out to the Greek ship and surround it. Once there, one of three commands would be given by the Dog Warrior's whistle: the first command being for the dogs to do nothing and just tread water in readiness until told otherwise by him. The second command would be for the dogs to either grab an arm of a person swimming or grab clothing and hold the swimmer in the same position in the water, where the Dog Warrior directed. The third command was a last resort and a most deadly one, where the dogs would swim beneath the surface and when they sensed a person exhaling, which they could do very easily, they would grab a leg with their powerful jaws and pull the swimmer beneath the waves until the victim would cease their underwater struggle for life.

Agrar had also selected three Men of Arms to go with him, each specialising in one weapon, these being the sword, spear and bow. The swordsman and spearman would accompany Agrar to the ship, the archer staying on the beach.

***

A small boat had been prepared at the shoreline for Agrar's boarding party. As he walked down to the boat he looked up at the morning sky where hundreds of noisy gulls were now acting strangely. They were all looking in the direction of the Greek ship as they repeatedly flew up from the sea high into the sky, squawking louder than they usually did. Agrar was instantly reminded of what Agrin had asked him the day before when he had said that the gulls were messengers from the Earth Goddess to the Sky God.

The dogs had also began to bark ferociously which now added an air of uncertainty and tension for everyone assembled.

The four men boarded the boat and were soon on their way out to the Greek ship followed by the swimming dogs.

The archer stood on the shoreline, accompanied by a small group of men who had prepared the boat for Agrar.

On board the Greek ship one of the crew sat at the stern which now faced landwards as the incoming tide pushed against it. As he fished, he called out to Pyris after noticing the approaching boat.

Agrar was still watching the gulls as they screeched and squawked overhead; they seemed to follow the boat he was in. Now he was convinced the Greeks had angered the Gods of Cornwall by bringing themselves here with their own Gods from afar – alien Gods bringing mischief and mayhem to the South West tip of this island.

Agrar's boat slowed as it approached the Greek ship which now revealed its grace and beauty to the chieftain and his men as they marvelled at its decoration and colourful finish in painted designs never seen by them before.

The dogs were now in place, each one equally spaced and circling the Greek ship.

The boat carrying the mighty chieftain now drew up aside the Greek vessel.

Pyris looked on nervously as he sensed the anger emanating from Agrar as the boat was tied up to his ship.

The Cornishmen quickly boarded the ship and stood in the middle of the decking forming a square of four men. Agrar stood in the front with the swordsman next to him, the Dog Warrior and spearman standing directly behind him.

A few of the Greek crew stood watching on the deck as Pyris approached Agrar to welcome him aboard. Pyris reached out his hand to Agrar but the chieftain just stood and stared, his spear now firmly clenched and his dagger ready at his side should he decide to use it.

"What sort of magic and curse have you brought upon us, Greek?" shouted Agrar.

Pyris had a small understanding of the language now being verbally projected at him and so he repeated only what he knew. "We come to trade, we want tin," he said and continued with other phrases known to him. "We are Greek, from far away," to which he pointed way over to the east where his homeland of Greece lay.

"Do you curse us, Greek?" shouted Agrar once more.

Soon all of the Greeks were on deck, most of them armed with swords and shields of bronze which had never been seen before by the Cornishmen.

Pyris now pleaded with Agrar to back off, pleading in his own tongue, but this sounded like a threat to Agrar.

The dogs were prepared for their master's command as they paddled in the cool clear waters of the bay.

Back on land the natives watched in anticipation, men and women now gathering on the beach and cliffs facing seawards towards the Greek ship.

Agrar and Pyris continued in a state of miscommunication and could not come to any understanding or agreement – it was a case of stalemate as the language barrier now frustrated Agrar in his anger and Pyris in his pleading with the mighty chieftain.

To add to the mayhem, the gulls had now moved seawards and were now directly over the Greek ship. Everyone looked up into the sky, both Cornishmen and Greeks.

Pyris commanded his men to put down their weapons which they did in a reluctant manner.

As this was happening, Agrar noticed a small statue towards the front of the ship, it was an image of the Greek God Poseidon who had given safe passage to the Greeks on their long voyage from the eastern Mediterranean. Uncontrollable anger now raged within Agrar as he raised his spear in readiness for combat as did his fellow Cornishmen. Agrar and his men formed a line and advanced towards the Greeks, pushing them towards the front of the ship.

The heartbeats of all the men increased, both Cornish and Greek, each taking a deeper breath than the last.

Agrar was convinced that the Greeks had come to curse them and let out a battle cry which was ferocious and sounded like the roar of ten lions.

The sky was clear and blue except for the gulls which appeared to be moving further out to sea. One single cloud in a hundred miles drifted through the heavens and came between the sun and the ship creating a dark shadow upon all aboard. This unnerved everyone and made one of the Greek sailors panic, he went over and started to climb one of the sail masts as he feared for his life. Everyone looked up at him and at the dark cloud above and as they did so, the figure of a woman emerged from below the decks and stood silently amongst them all. The dark cloud was pushed away by a sudden gust of wind and all on board were dazzled by the intense bright sunlight from above, each man putting his hands in front of his face to cover his eyes and those holding weapons dropping them as they did so.

As Agrar rubbed his eyes, the hairs on the back of his neck stood up and he remembered feeling as he had done the night before when his dream spirit had wandered the universe in search for his long lost wife. He lowered his hands, opened his eyes and as they cleared and focused he was greeted with the sight of a beautiful woman standing before him, her hair longer than before and her skin darker, but there in front of him stood Alvaria, his wife, whom he had not seen for six years.

CHAPTER 6

Alvaria had been badly treated by her captors six years since. Her heart had broken at this time due to the combination of extreme cruelty together with the separation from her husband and son, who she loved so very much. She had been driven to the point of collapse and at this time her memory had left her, heart and soul, leaving her an empty shell emotionally.

Pyris and his people were known as Caspitarians and their bitter enemies, the Tantarians had been Alvaria's captors. She had been rescued and taken in by the Caspitarians where she had taught Pyris some of the language of Bronze Age Cornwall.

***

Both the Greeks and the men of Cornwall backed away to the edges of the ship as Agrar and Alvaria stood facing one another, their eyes directly focused on each other's. The light breeze stopped and all was silent as the minutes ticked by. Agrar stood wondering why Alvaria seemed not to know him, but as he was thinking this, memory triggers were now firing deep within Alvaria's mind. The two figures walked towards each other, the sun directly overhead, as their shadows now vanished. Agrar put out his right arm and wrapped his large strong hand around Alvaria's female left hand.

Suddenly, a burst of energy exploded between them both, a vibration shot through the ship and was transferred into the sea, sending the dogs away from the ship in confusion. Agrar embraced his wife and in an instant her memory was restored. All the pain suffered throughout the years of separation melted away.

"Agrar, is that you?"

"Yes, my wife, it is I and you have been returned to me by the Gods of this land."

Alvaria looked around and saw all the men watching, she looked down at the decking and gazed at Agrar's spear. "What has happened here, husband, and why are your weapons aboard?" She looked over to Pyris and said, "These people rescued me, husband, and made me well. It is they who have brought me home."

Agrar's mind now started to recollect what Mendax the Dream Teller had told him. He had only told Agrar that he must go to the Greek ship and that was all. He did not foresee Alvaria aboard but knew questions would be answered for Agrar should he venture to the craft moored in the bay.

The couple embraced in such a way that they became one through their love for each other and all on deck felt relieved from the tension and hostility that had existed only minutes before.

***

All these events answered one dream's questions, but not those of the other, now forgotten by Agrar, of the sea claiming his and Alvaria's son Agrin.

"Tell me of Pyris and his people," asked Agrar.

"They are good men and women who have looked after me as if I were one of their own."

Alvaria told the mighty chieftain of all the events that had happened to her over the past six years and as she did so, both Greek and Cornishmen surrounded them both to listen. She spoke first in Cornish and then in Greek as she explained to everyone.

The dogs had now swum back to the shore and the Greek mariner who had climbed the sail mast was now transfixed with something way out to sea, something unknown as yet to all on board.

When Alvaria had finished her tale to all, Agrar spoke to her. "Tell Pyris that I was mistaken about him and my thoughts of the Greeks cursing our land."

"But why did you think this, my husband?"

"I will explain everything to you later, my wife."

After Alvaria had spoken to Pyris he walked over to Agrar and the two men embraced, the chieftain humbled himself and showed respect by kneeling down and kissing the feet of Pyris the Greek. This was an ancient and spiritual custom of Agrar and the people of Cornwall who considered the feet holy to them. They were the root of a man's spirit just as a tree has roots which hold it strong in the ground so would a man's feet upon the ground. As the roots of a tree would feed it as it grew and matured, the bare feet of men would draw energy from the earth during life and also a build-up of negative energy or spirit could be neutralised by the feet and the power of water. Just as a lightning conductor transfers and routes the energy of lightning to the ground, so could these ancient people from the Bronze Age control unwanted energies within themselves through their feet.

Agrar stood up straight, he felt uplifted for the Greeks had not brought bad spirits or a curse with them but the opposite was true. Wine was passed around and at this time all seemed well.

***

As everyone on deck celebrated, the Greek sailor who was still high up on the sail mast began to shout excitedly.

"What is he saying, Alvaria?"

"Ships, Agrar, he has seen ships."

Alvaria spoke to Pyris who explained to her that the fleet of ships would carry the tin back to his homeland.

Agrar now realised why the gulls had been acting so strangely and why they had flown over the Greek ship and out to sea. They had mistaken the Greek armada for fishing boats which had excited them this day.

Everyone looked out towards the horizon, waiting for the appearance of the ships. The original fleet was of thirty ships but now only twenty-five remained as bad weather and pirates had claimed five Greek ships on their voyage to Cornwall. The Greeks had anticipated losses and knew that the return voyage would be a perilous one as the ships would appear low in the water showing that they were carrying precious cargo. These ships would be easy targets for their enemies and pirates. It had been estimated that only ten fully loaded ships were needed to return home for enough weapons and armour to be made. The Caspitarians possessed much copper and in proportion required far less tin as bronze was made from nine parts copper and one part tin.

Agrar and Alvaria once more embraced, their bodies entwined together and Alvaria's soft sweet voice asked Agrar of their son. "What is our son like, husband?"

"He has your eyes, determination and spirit," replied Agrar.

"Can we now go ashore and be with him together?"

"Yes, we must go back to the village, I will give instructions to Pyris to follow us later when the Greek fleet has arrived and have dropped their anchors."

The small boat made its way back to the shore carrying Agrar and Alvaria. Many people had now gathered together upon the beach to await their chieftain's command once he had returned and to know the outcome of his visit to the Greek ship.

The Greek fleet was just about visible from the beach and a loud roar came from all who had gathered. Agrar stood up in the boat as it approached the beach and blew on his horn to signal that all was well.

Agrin was still in the village and had done just as his father had commanded him. All Agrar's weapons and bronze implements had been checked and maintained to the highest standard. He had even sharpened his father's bronze razor and polished his father's bronze mirror. Personal grooming was very important to Agrar and his tribe, the Agrarian people.

***

As the boat carrying Agrar came ashore, its underside made contact with the wet sand and a jolt was felt by all on board. The boat was soon surrounded by many people who looked on to see their chieftain reunited with his wife. Soon, all had climbed out of the boat and were standing on the soft sand beneath them. Alvaria and Agrar both dropped to their knees and shouted out in gratitude to their gods.

"Oh God of the Sea and of my ancestors, I thank thee for returning my wife," said Agrar.

"Oh mighty Poseidon, God of the Sea, I thank thee for this day and for bringing me home," said Alvaria.

Agrar turned to Alvaria and said, "Wife, this is a word that is not known to me."

"Dear husband, we people of this land refer to the gods as God of the Sea, Sky, Earth & so on but the Greeks have names for their gods."

"This is strange for me to hear and accept, my wife, as we are mere men and women, all mortals with mortal names so surely it is wrong to give a God a name, names are for us, the Agrarian and also for earthly things."

"Agrar, dearest husband of mine, I am sure that in time you will accept God names, but if you don't it matters not, for a God is a God by any name or title."

"Yes, Alvaria, this is true. Come, let us go to the village and see our son, Agrin."

Hand in hand, they walked back to the village with many people following, young and old, in joyous mood and spirit for today everyone felt happy for their mighty chieftain Agrar.

As they walked, Alvaria could taste the sea air of her homeland and a breeze as gentle as a child welcomed her home as her soft skin felt its presence. The rhythm of her heart now changed in anticipation of seeing her son of whom she had lost all memory until today. Her hair danced as she walked, increasing her pace as the village neared.

Agrin was stood in the centre of the village when he became aware of the approaching sounds of many people coming towards him. He was soon surrounded by a large crowd who stood back as into view came Agrar and Alvaria still holding hands. The boy rubbed his eyes as his mother and father approached him, thinking it was all a dream again but no, this was no dream. Agrin ran to his parents with a new word ready to be given flight by his tongue "Mother, Mother," he cried, "Is it you?"

"Yes, my son, it is I, your mother, returned to you and your father from far away across the waters."

The three embraced, each one's heart melting in a sea of happiness. Agrin's eyes were as bright as could ever be.

CHAPTER 7

The fleet of Greek ships were now nearing the pilot ship which Pyris had captained and which now lay in the bay awaiting them. Pyris and his crew felt relieved now and at ease for their fellow countrymen were now arriving on the Cornish coast. These ships were different from the native ones of this island, the shape and decoration was beyond the imagination of Agrar and his people. The ships were dropping their anchors and forming an impressive armada all around Pyris and his crew who continued to watch in awe and fascination. Once all the ships were tied up, the captains of each vessel would come and talk with Pyris and listen to what he had agreed to with the tin traders ashore. Pyris was glad that all was now well, the fleet had arrived and Alvaria had been reunited with her people and family.

Agrar felt happy and now favoured the Greeks in their quest for tin.

***

Agrar's heart and soul now danced and his spirit was lifted as high as any man's could be. He sent a messenger to the valley of Lupax to invite Mendax, the Dream Teller in celebration of this day.

Alvaria sat inside the home that she had not seen for six years and as she did so even more memories came flooding back to her. She marvelled at Agrin, her son and could not take her eyes off him. Mother and son talked for ages, Agrin was most curious about the land she had just come from with the Greeks. Alvaria's love was now rekindled for her son.

Agrar stood outside and gave orders to working groups to start taking the timbers onto the beach. Each group was given specific tasks which suited their skills and abilities. Men, women and children, each playing an important role in preparation for the construction of the jetty where the tin would be loaded onto the Greek ships.

He also made sure the tin was safely in its secret storehouse which was two caves close to the village. This was a place kept secret to avoid the theft of this highly valued commodity. The tin had already been melted into ingots and stockpiled ready for such a time as this.

He gave orders that he was not to be disturbed until later that afternoon as he wished to spend time alone with Alvaria and Agrin.

Food was prepared for him and soon he was inside the roundhouse with his family.

"What have you been talking about?" he asked Alvaria and Agrin.

"Father, do you know much about the Greeks?"

"No, my son, just that they come from far away, speak in a strange tongue and dress very differently than we do."

"Do you think we will ever see their land, Father?"

"I think I will not, Agrin but maybe when you are older and a mighty chieftain and tin trader then maybe you will one day set out across the sea and visit the Greeks and take the tin to them. You can see the marvels of where they live and buy many wondrous things to bring back to Cornwall."

"Yes, Father, I will."

Agrin and Alvaria both looked at one another and smiled as Agrin's mind imagined future adventures in his life.

The hours quickly passed as the three talked and told tales of past and future.

The short figure of a man approached the village, it was the Dream Teller, Mendax. He made his way through the village and arrived at Agrar's house where he stood in the doorway.

Agrar stood up, welcoming him into the house. "Mendax, please come in." He introduced his wife and son and said, "Thank you, Mendax, for telling me that the answer to my dream awaited me on board the Greek ship."

"That is true, mighty chieftain, but even I, with my power and abilities, did not foresee Alvaria's return."

"You are too modest, Mendax, now tell me is all well now with our land and people?"

"I can only answer what I have foreseen and so will return in a day or two with the answer to your question, Agrar."

Agrar accepted the Dream Teller's answer and bid him good day.

Mendax made his way back home. He knew that things were not well and that tragedy waited in the wings for Agrar to soon experience.

How could Mendax tell of such a thing on this good day of celebration for Agrar's family?

As he reached the top of the hill before descending into the valley to his house, he sat and looked out to sea. The Greek fleet lay below him, afloat on a shimmering silver sea. He took off his sandals and sat with his legs bent with the soles of his feet and the palms of his hands placed upon the lush grass. The earth energies were strong here where his body made contact with Mother Earth. With his eyes shut he could still see danger lying in wait for Agrin.

***

Out at sea, the ships' captains had gathered on board Pyris' ship and were making plans for their return voyage back to Greece. It was decided that two ships per day would be loaded with tin and set sail for home. The ships would not travel back to Greece as a fleet but in pairs with a day's separation between each sailing.

A few of the captains did not favour this idea but it would certainly be safer in some respects, these being that should a mighty storm break out at sea then only one or two ships would be put in danger. Also, if any of the ships were attacked by pirates, they would probably be happy with that conquest and sell the captured tin to the highest bidder, leaving the remaining ships to sail home unharmed or without hindrance.

The hundreds of seagulls that had excitedly flown out to sea to greet the Greek fleet had dispersed in disappointment whilst the Sky God had looked down in amusement at them.

***

Agrar and his family emerged from the roundhouse into the late afternoon sun. People were hurrying about, to and fro, happy in the knowledge that great wealth would be shared between them all. They had come from far and wide as the news had started to spread across Cornwall of the ships from another sea with men aboard who were different to any seen before.

Although the Greeks had come to trade for tin, many other items would be offered to them over the next few days, such things as amber from the south east of the island which had been made into beautiful necklaces and jewellery consisting of beads and even drinking vessels which were considered as very high status. Amber was highly revered back in the Bronze Age and would find its way all over Europe and beyond, just as tin did three thousand years ago.

"Father, can we go and greet the Greeks down at the beach?"

"Yes, Agrin, we will go soon."

"Mother, will you come as well?"

"No, Agrin, I have much to catch up on here and need to rekindle old friendships with some of the womenfolk here."

"Okay, Mother."

Alvaria was soon surrounded by old friends and talked with them.

Agrar turned to his son and asked, "Have you tended my spears and arrows this day, son?"

"Yes, Father, your spear will stop a giant and your arrows will fly true and far to wherever you direct them."

"Good, then today you will be my spear bearer, so go now and choose one and walk with me with pride in the knowledge that you are an Agrarian, the mightiest people in all the land."

Agrin rushed back inside the roundhouse and selected a spear whilst his father talked with some of the village men.

CHAPTER 8

At the beach, many people had gathered including over 200 Greek mariners eager to load their ships with tin and set sail back to their homeland where weapons of bronze could be cast.

Both the Greeks and the Cornishmen looked warily at each other, analysing the different appearances in physical form and clothing. Suspicion was still in the Cornishmen's minds as in the past, many had come from afar, bearing weapons upon the tin trading community of this area.

A few men tried to communicate with each other but mainly the Greeks stayed with the Greeks and the Cornish with the Cornish.

Pyris awaited Agrar's appearance. Next to him stood Aquilla, the captain of the fleet. The two men had inspected the large timbers which would make up the loading jetty that would stretch out to sea and take several days to complete. The Greeks would assist in the task and perhaps a bond would form between them and the men of Cornwall.

"Pyris, what sort of man is their chieftain?" asked Aquilla. He spoke in Greek, but like Pyris, knew many words taught to them both by Alvaria.

"He is a proud man and one of honour," replied Pyris.

"Does he trust us yet or is his mind still clouded by past events; by travellers like us coming from afar?"

"It was our enemies who last came here and took his wife Alvaria as well as helping themselves to the tin."

"Yes, you are right, and it was, I think, more than just luck that we rescued her from the Tantarians, I am sure the Gods had a hand in this matter."

"Perhaps, my friend, perhaps," said Pyris.

"Yes, Pyris, the Gods and us must learn more of this strange land before we leave as I sense through my earth spirit that this land, although very different from ours and slightly primitive in some ways, will give us much and we will have many wonderful experiences here."

Aquilla and Pyris walked along together observing all who had gathered. Some of the men were play fighting on the golden sand which lay underfoot. Others were swimming, now in water far colder than they normally experienced.

A young boy wandered amongst all that was happening. He had no real name and was called by everyone that knew him locally as Stick. He spoke very rarely and no-one had ever seen him eating which probably accounted for him being so thin. This combined with his very dark brown skin, meant he could easily be compared to a stick lying on the ground. He was five feet tall, his hair always a mess and his hands and feet slightly large in proportion to his body. No one knew his age but he looked like a typical boy between twelve and fourteen years of age.

Another reason for his name could be related to the fact that he was very knowledgeable about trees and timber. He knew all the best woods for certain tasks and although not a great speaker of words he could be very useful to the village. Another strange thing about him was that he had a tattoo of a raven under his left armpit, no one knew why or what this symbolised.

Stick and Agrin were good friends, but kept this a secret as some people thought the boy a bad omen as he was different from them. Even Agrar knew the boy but did not favour him much and had instructed Agrin to limit their playtime together.

Stick lived alone and was thought of by most people as an orphan and outcast. He continued wandering about, totally unnoticed by all.

***

Agrar approached the beach; at his side was Agrin, his right hand tightly gripping the shaft of one of his father's finest spears. A procession of people followed who were flanked by twenty dogs, ten on either side of them, each controlled by the Dog Warrior whose bald head glistened with sweat in the afternoon sun.

Agrar raised his arm and signalled his people to halt. He could see all who had gathered on the beach in front of him, he raised the horn to his lips and blew out a sound of welcome to the Greeks.

Within a few minutes, every Cornishman for miles around joined in the welcome and as the sound spread across the land, beacons were lit on high places to add to this special day.

Agrar walked with his people onto the beach and made a beeline for Pyris and Aquilla. The swimmers came ashore and the men play-fighting stopped as the Bronze Age chieftain approached.

Alvaria would follow her husband and son soon and would translate between the men of Greece and Cornwall.

Agrar and Agrin stood in front of Pyris and Aquilla, Agrin directly in front of Pyris who looked down at the boy and smiled. Agrar stood facing Aquilla who had dressed for the occasion by wearing full battle dress which he thought would impress the chieftain – it was an impressive sight indeed.

Aquilla stood erect – he was a fine looking man and his adornment of cloth, leather and bronze was an awesome sight to the people of Bronze Age Britain.

At this time, the native peoples were only now just casting swords for weaponry and had never seen what looked like a Man of Bronze. His bronze helmet hid most of his face but Agrar could see Aquilla's piercing blue eyes now scrutinising him. Agrar walked around him and was very impressed as the Greek also had upon himself a beautifully decorated bronze breastplate. This was made of a softer bronze than his spear and sword and had been hand beaten into shape, profiling the strong looking torso of Aquilla.

Agrar pointed to the shield and had it handed to him by the Greek. Shields of Britain were made of wood so to see a large bronze shield was a most interesting sight. He handed back the shield and almost envied Aquilla's impressive appearance. A few words were exchanged between the two men and Pyris requested that some Greek sailors fetch some matting and lay it upon the sand.

Pyris spoke to Aquilla who removed his helmet, breastplate and weapons and laid them down on the matting now in place. Agrar, Pyris and Aquilla sat on the matting and tried to communicate.

As this was happening, Agrin caught sight of Stick wandering around on his own as usual. He placed the spear down behind his father and wandered over to his friend. As he did so, his father glanced over, keeping a watchful eye on him. He made a hand signal to his son which the boy knew and understood. It was telling him not to wander off out of sight.

The three men sat and drank a toast to their trading deal.

Aquilla could not miss the way Agrar had taken a big interest in the sword, helmet and shield that lay on the matting in front of him.

CHAPTER 9

"Hey, Stick, what are you up to?"

"Oh, you know me," replied the boy, "I'm just being nosy and curious. These Greeks are an interesting people don't you think, Agrin?"

"Yes, I agree, and I hope all goes well with the tin trading deal they are agreeing with my father."

The boys sat on the left side of the beach and both gazed in awe at the armada of ships anchored in the bay they had swum in since young boys.

"Do you think the Greeks would let us on board one of their ships?" asked Agrin.

Stick just shrugged his shoulders and went into his usual silent mode.

Agrin liked the boy even though many others, including his own father, did not. He also knew by the way Stick sometimes looked at him that sometime in his life bad things had happened to him. At times there was a great sadness in his eyes and Agrin wanted in his heart to help him and pledged an oath to himself that one day he would.

"This is truly a great day!" exclaimed Agrin.

"Mmm," replied Stick.

"It is, my friend, yes, a great day for us all."

"Okay, if you say so Agrin," came a disgruntled reply.

"Well, just look around us, all the excitement, the Greeks and the ships, and my mother has returned to us safely." Agrin paused as Stick yawned heavily.

"Oh, and one other thing."

"Oh, yes, what?"

"I am sat next to my best friend."

Stick turned and looked at Agrin. "Do you mean that?"

"Oh, yes, of course I do."

Stick was not expecting such a statement and said, "Agrin, you will one day be our chieftain and it is then that you will forget me as your friend."

"No, Stick, I will not." He reached over and held Stick's left hand. "You will always be my friend, Stick, I promise."

With that, Stick smiled, which was indeed a rarity.

The two boys suddenly burst out laughing together.

"I better go now," said Agrin.

"Okay, Agrin, see you soon."

Agrin wandered back over to where his father and the two Greeks, Pyris and Aquilla, sat with one another, the men now looking at ease with one another.

As the hours passed, more and more of the Greeks and Cornishmen approached one another and tried to communicate.

***

Alvaria arrived at the beach with some of the womenfolk from the village. She would act as interpreter for the many questions from Agrar and the Greeks.

Agrin ran to meet her and walked with her the last one hundred yards to where Agrar, Pyris and Aquilla now stood waiting.

As the evening drew in, much was said by all whilst some of the Greeks had erected tents further up the beach and would stay on land until their ships needed to be loaded with tin. Many small boats lay dotted about the beach; these had ferried the Greek mariners ashore.

The larger ships out at sea would at all times have at least two crew men aboard.

***

Tomorrow would be a busy day in which the loading jetty construction would begin. Greeks and Cornishmen working together, each with their own customs and Gods. These Gods would watch over them but had agreed not to interfere in any matter that may arise, be it good or bad.

***

Gradually, people started to make their way home. The Dog Warrior had exercised his dogs this afternoon, getting many attentive looks of admiration from the Greeks. He returned with his twenty dogs to his home which lay just outside the village.

Stick had soon disappeared out of sight after talking with Agrin on the beach.

Agrar bid the Greeks goodnight and together with his wife and son he too made his way home to the village where a fresh boar had been slain and was now roasting over an open fire.

Pyris and Aquilla would return to their ships respectively.

"I will see you at first light, Pyris," said Aquilla.

"Yes, that you will, and together we will do all we can to speed up the building of the jetty and the loading of tin."

"You seem tense, my friend."

"Yes, Aquilla, I fear for our homeland and its people."

"We have travelled far, Pyris and for many weeks. All we can now do is pray to the Gods that the Tantarians, our evil enemies, are still not ready to attack our lands and kill our people."

"Yes, Aquilla, and tonight I will pray to the mighty Zeus himself and pay homage by making a sacrifice."

"Come, my friend, let us return to our ships."

Several small ferry boats made their way out to sea in the direction of the Greek armada. Pyris felt a little homesick as he gazed up at the stars in the evening sky. How he missed his wife and daughter and as he thought of them his heart ached and tears formed in the corner of each eye. But Pyris knew that if he and his countrymen were successful they would save Caspitaria and all who lived there.

He reached his ship accompanied by two other men; they were soon on board where Pyris went directly to where he kept all his belongings. He looked through them, wanting to find something suitable and worthy to sacrifice to Zeus and Poseidon. After some time Pyris decided what he would sacrifice; a decorative dagger given to him by his king. He went on deck and walked over to the side of the ship that we know as starboard. A prayer was said in which he offered this most treasured possession but just as he reached over the side of the ship a voice entered into his head, saying, 'Is this really your most valued possession?'

He noticed that around his outstretched arm which was ready to deliver the dagger unto the sea, was an armband and bracelet. His wife had made and decorated the leather armband and his daughter had made the fabric bracelet for him before he had left his homeland as a reminder of their undying love for him.

Pyris was now in turmoil as his heart and his head battled in trying to convince him to sacrifice either the dagger or the armband and bracelet.

He let go of the dagger, for in that moment he realised what was really of great value to him and so the Gods would know of his sacrifice. The dagger was now of no consequence as it made its way down to the seabed, it's true value only being one of possession.

Pyris now undid the armband and bracelet and removed them both. He held them tenderly before kissing them.

"Oh mighty Poseidon, God of the Sea and Zeus, God of all others, accept these as offerings to you. He once again extended his arm out over the water as his thoughts once more turned to his family. His hand relaxed its grip and both objects fell onto the water, slowly floating away into the distance.

He had indeed at that moment sacrificed his most treasured possessions, not of gold, silver or jewels but of leather and cloth, and as he stared out over the sea he realised that he had performed an act of true love and sacrifice. His heart sang out and his spirit was quenched with truth and love, making him happy and content.

Today, Pyris had learnt a true lesson in life, together with its true meaning.

CHAPTER 10

The next day arrived and no sooner had dawn started to break, than people set to work upon the beach. The tide was receding and every able bodied person would help first to erect the vertical timber stanchions which would support the upper planked decking of the jetty. Men of this time were used to hard physical work especially the tin traders of the area. As the tide ebbed away out to sea, vertical logs were appearing as holes in the wet sand were hurriedly dug to house the jetty supports.

The Greeks and Cornish worked well together, all eager to now co-operate with each other in this vital task.

Agrin had gone down onto the beach to watch and help if asked.

Agrar and Alvaria were spending some time together before going down to the beach later that day. They had not lain together for six years and would now make love with each other many times.

***

People started to arrive from afar, some to help and others to sell or trade their wares.

High upon the nearby hills overlooking the valley of Lupax sat the Dream Teller, Mendax. He would later go down to the beach as he was curious and wanted to meet the Greek mariners. He also knew that tragedy was coming to Agrar and Alvaria if his interpretation of the chieftain's dreams were correct.

"Boy, go and fetch water for drinking," boomed out a voice from one of the visiting helpers.

"Go on, boy, we are thirsty, hurry up!"

Agrin was amused at this request and went immediately to fetch water. Whilst doing so he smiled to himself as he realised that the man did not know he was the son of the Agrarian people's chieftain, Agrar.

"Here you are, water, just as you asked," said Agrin.

"Well done, boy, now stay out of the way and come back with more water later."

Agrin did not recognise the man but as he looked rather fierce, he just smiled at him and moved away.

***

As the day passed, two impressive rows of vertical uprights could be seen emerging from the sand standing fast and strong ready for the next stage in the construction of the tin loading jetty. After six hours, the tide started to turn and was coming slowly inwards towards the shore.

Mendax had come down to the beach and was wandering amongst all that was happening. He saw Agrin and made his way towards the boy.

"Ah, Agrin, my boy, is your father here?"

"No, not yet, but I am sure he will come soon."

Mendax looked at the boy and said, "I think it would be wise if you stayed away from the water this day, Agrin." Although he was a dream teller, he was also a psychic and knew that events far beyond his control were soon to happen. He could not interfere in the affairs of a mortal's destiny but was allowed to give advice when he thought necessary.

***

Pyris and Aquilla were also starting to wonder where Agrar was, when suddenly the sound of the chieftain's horn was heard approaching. Everyone on the beach stopped and watched the arrival of Agrar and Alvaria as they made their way down to where all the labours of the morning had taken place. Food was brought to everyone and they all rested, ate and drank.

As Pyris took food he looked down at his right forearm which was now without the armband and bracelet it had worn with such pride and love. *Where have they floated to?* he thought to himself, *and has Zeus accepted the offering to him by Pyris the Greek?*

Aquilla sat next to him. He was a quiet man but at all times was analysing all that was happening around him. He was most impressed at the way both his fellow countrymen and men of Cornwall had co-operated and worked this day. Both he and Pyris could not wait to set sail once more and return home to defeat the Tantarians should they attack their homeland.

Agrar and Alvaria called over to Agrin to sit with them and the two Greek Captains. Soon, many questions were answered as Alvaria interpreted between the Cornish and the Greeks.

The Greeks had rescued Alvaria and although she had lost her memory they had recognised her language as the tongue of the Cornish and had hoped that one day this could be used to their advantage and now, on this very day, it had. They had treated her well over the years and she had been greatly admired by many of the Greek women for her beauty, humility and compassion for all. Many men had also admired her beauty and had tried in vain to gain her affections, but Alvaria had never taken an interest in any of them. Perhaps the Gods had played a part in this, as they knew that one day she and Agrar would be reunited once again.

As they all sat together, an atmosphere of friendship and co-operation was felt by all.

Through Alvaria, Aquilla asked about Agrar's ancestry, to which he replied, "Our ancestors came from the other side of these waters many generations ago, they too had worked with metals and heard of this island and its tin. They decided to come and settle here."

Aquilla asked Agrar where, geographically, his ancestors had lived in relation to Cornwall. "A land far warmer than this, where tin could also be found, a land which was to the south west and on the northern shores of the middle sea." Agrar was describing southern Spain and the Mediterranean Sea, Aquilla had recognised where he was describing and spoke.

"We have much in common, chieftain of this land, as the middle sea that you described is where we have come from. Your ancestors lived to the west, whereas we have our homeland on the other side of the middle sea, far to the east of it."

A look of astonishment came over Agrar's face as these Greeks had sailed past his ancestors' homeland and in his mind he thought back to the stories handed over from father to son and of the tales from that place in Southern Spain long, long ago.

Alvaria was pleased that her husband now accepted these men as brothers.

Pyris asked, "What of the dogs that were here on the beach yesterday, accompanied by the one you call the Dog Warrior?"

"Those dogs were brought with the ancestors to this land," replied Alvaria.

"They are such fine looking animals and so intelligent," replied Pyris.

"As are we," laughed Agrar and as Alvaria translated to all those around, everyone joined in the laughter.

***

Soon work started again but this would be restricted as the tide line was gradually creeping in. A lot the of the planked decking could now be prepared for later and soon every man was hard at his labour. The sky was becoming darker this afternoon and the light breeze was now amplified into a strong wind at times. The sea became choppy and as the tide was an incoming one some of the waves were now pushing hard upon the beach.

Agrin had wandered over to a large pile of logs and timber. He had been fascinated by all the events of the day and was now imagining the logs as an interesting adventure playground.

Agrar and Alvaria were some way away when shouts went out from some of the men on the beach. People turned and looked seawards where a larger than normal wave was making its way inland towards them all.

Agrin's mind was on the imaginary adventure he was now playing out upon the logs and timber.

"Agrin!" shouted both the boy's mother and father only to have the strength and sound of their voices drowned out by the strong wind taking it in the other direction.

Pyris and Aquilla could see Agrin some way down the beach and started running towards him as the giant wave was becoming larger and faster and was only moments from where Agrin played.

Agrar and Alvaria were now also running towards the boy as the wind increased its power, almost knocking Agrin over as he played. He regained his balance and turned to see the giant menacing wave heading straight towards him. He froze for a moment and turned his back on the wave as he desperately tried to jump from the logs. It was too late for the boy, who was hit from behind by the powerful wall of water. The force of the water sent Agrin's body spinning beneath the waves together with the logs he had been playing upon which were sent out in all directions in an uncontrollable way. Agrin had managed to hold his breath as he entered the water but as he floundered to gain control one of the logs crashed into him, rendering him unconscious.

The giant wave now receded, dragging the boy and the logs outwards from the shore. The wave had been so large that an immense volume of water rushed back from the sand, dragging away anything in its path.

Agrar and Alvaria stood silently in bewilderment, waiting awhile for the sea to settle.

Pyris and Aquilla arrived and all four looked at one another in desperation. There was no sign of Agrin as the sea calmed itself and a terror now entered the minds of the chieftain and his wife as they leapt into the water, searching in vain for their son Agrin.

CHAPTER 11

Mendax had been observing the events of the day from afar and he wondered why the Gods had decided to take Agrin into the sea. The boy was innocent and his parents, Agrar and Alvaria, were worthy to have a son like him. In fact, Mendax often felt through his spirit that all three of them were favoured by the Gods and born unto this land by the Gods as they were noble and honest with a caring nature towards all men, women and children who lived in this community.

***

Agrar had always honoured his Gods as his father had before him. He also told stories of the ancestors and the natural Gods of the Earth, Sea and Sky. Agrin loved these stories and they had instilled in him many good qualities – why would these Gods now take the boy on this day? Especially after his father had often paid them homage and made offerings to them.

***

What of Pyris the evening before? He had made the ultimate sacrifice to Zeus and Poseidon by firstly dropping his prized dagger into the sea after realising it was the illusory power of possession that made him regard it as precious.

Pyris had now realised that the armband and bracelet he wore were of more value than anything else to him.

How could any Gods whether Greek or Cornish be angered at this time and make, of all people, a boy the target and victim of their rage?

Mendax, Pyris and Agrar were now confused by this tragic event, each trying to work out which God had been angered. They could not know the truth, for it was not an obvious one to them.

A demon God had been summoned that day, but not a God of the Greeks nor of the Cornish, no, it was another God, one evoked by somebody else, but who and why?

***

Desperation took flight in the hearts of Agrar and Alvaria as they searched the waters for their son. They both searched the shallower part of the sea whilst Aquilla and Pyris swam out to search the deeper ones. The best swimmers of both the Cornish and the Greeks swam out far to sea in their quest to locate the boy.

As all this was taking place, Agrin's body drifted lifelessly beneath the waves; there was no sign of movement or consciousness coming from him.

As the minutes passed away a new sense of hopelessness haunted Agrar's mind. His emotions were sent into total spasms of chaos. He waded through the water up to his knees and suddenly stood still whilst looking skywards. The chieftain removed his lower garments below the waist and with his left hand he directed his urine at the sea as he held himself. "God of the Sea, I piss upon you this day," he shouted up to the heavens and continued to urinate until his bladder was empty. He hurled further insults at the Gods as he knelt down in the sea whilst punching hard into the water.

Alvaria knelt down beside him and put her arm around him to comfort her husband. She had been returned to him, but now his son had been taken, but why?

Five minutes had now elapsed, but to Agrar it felt like five hours.

Pyris and Aquilla looked at one another and swam back to shore. The two of them were also confused as to why the boy Agrin should be claimed by the freak wave, especially as they had travelled thousands of miles across a sea and an ocean, arriving safely in Cornwall despite all the dangers they had faced on their voyage from their motherland of Greece.

The two men walked over to Agrar, Pyris once more worried that he may blame them for coming here and cursing him.

As Agrar and his wife both knelt in the sea, his eyes looked up at the two Greeks as he spoke through the heart and not the head.

"Ask your men to keep searching for my son, please, Pyris."

Alvaria interpreted his words to the sympathetic Greek.

"I shall, Agrar, and our men will not stop until your son is found." As Pyris spoke these words he feared inside that this may not happen.

***

Everyone was now searching in the vicinity in which the wave had hit Agrin and dragged him out to sea.

Way over to the right where the vertical timbers had been erected, a slight figure of a person had gone unnoticed by all. It was Stick; he had climbed up on one of the stanchions that stood furthest out to sea and was now looking down into the water. He knew something of the sea but most importantly he understood the direction of the strong undercurrents beneath it. He too carried a small signalling horn with him and now blew upon it as hard as he could. This attracted the attention of some of the searchers.

Stick dived into the sea. After twenty seconds the boy resurfaced. Two heads were visible in the water, Stick had found Agrin and rescued his lifeless body from the depths. He swam as hard as he could whilst holding onto the boy.

"Agrin, Agrin, wake up," he cried as they headed back to shore. "Agrin, my friend, please wake up," he continued to yell.

A few people had worked out that it was Agrin in the distance being helped ashore by his friend Stick.

As this happened a roar of voices trumpeted into the air and a mass exodus of men headed over towards the two boys.

"Agrar, look!" said Alvaria.

Upon hearing this, Agrar immediately stood up and together with the Greeks they started to hurry over towards the stanchions.

Stick was halfway to the shore when some of the other rescuers reached him and Agrin. Two big strong men took over from Stick as they were more powerful swimmers and rushed Agrin's body up onto the sand where they gently laid his body down upon the ground.

Stick's feet could now touch the sand beneath him and he stood silently watching as tears formed in his eyes. He begged the Gods to help his friend. "O, God of this land, please do not let my friend die, this I beg of you, please." *I think the Sea God has done this by mistake*, he thought to himself. But now Agrin was on dry land, perhaps another God would help, but how?

***

A large crowd surrounded Agrin's body, all looking down upon him with sorrow in their eyes.

The crowd parted as Agrar and Alvaria arrived, immediately kneeling next to their son's pale, ashen and lifeless body. Agrar held the boy's cold body against his chest and sobbed.

Suddenly, something very strange and totally unexpected started to happen.

Pyris whispered into the ear of Alvaria saying these words, "Alvaria, you have known me for many years, take heed of what I now say, as it is the only hope of saving your son."

Alvaria's attention now hung on every word being spoken to her whilst Agrar was blinded by his grief and could not see or hear anything as he held tightly to Agrin's body.

Pyris finished telling Alvaria what he had to say and turned and spoke to his fellow countrymen in Greek. After he had done so, he looked back at Alvaria and nodded his head at her.

Four of the biggest and strongest Greeks came forward and without warning took hold of Agrar to restrain him as another two Greeks took hold of Agrin and laid him belly down upon the sand, his head to one side.

Agrar struggled and shouted out, "Agrarians, help me and gather all these cursed Greeks up! They are not to be trusted anymore."

As his fellow Cornishmen were going to obey his orders, Alvaria spoke to them. "Men of Cornwall, I ask you

70

not to obey your chieftain just this once please, I beg of you."

Confusion was rife amongst Agrar's people and so Alvaria spoke once again. "The Greeks say they may be able to help my son, although what they are about to do to him will appear strange or wrong to us."

"But we must obey our chieftain!" shouted one man.

Alvaria reached over to her husband and took his dagger. She held it against herself and said, "Then I would rather kill myself than not let the Greeks give Agrin his only chance for life."

Everyone gathered knew her words were genuine and that she would rather kill herself and join her son in the afterlife than not let the Greeks try their plan, whatever it may be.

CHAPTER 12

Whilst this was happening, the crowd were ordered to step back ten paces.

Agrar watched on, his mind full of rage and anger towards the Greeks who were restraining him. Alvaria stood next to him. A large arena of sand surrounded the now solitary body of Agrin. Pyris and eleven other Greeks, making twelve men in all, stood in a line next to the boy's body. Pyris began to march on the spot as one by one the other eleven Greeks followed his steps until they were all in sync. Pyris whistled and marched forward towards the body of Agrin, the line of men reached the body and one by one marched over him whilst placing one foot heavily between the shoulder blades of Agrin.

Agrar looked on in horror and screamed out obscenities at the Greeks and naturally the large crowd did not feel at ease with this either. A few Cornishmen stepped forward only to be told to get back by Alvaria as she once more focused on the dagger she was holding against herself.

Once the twelve men had marched over Agrin's body they turned around to once more face him. Pyris looked slightly anxious, he walked over to Agrin and turned the boy's head to face the other way. Again, they marched over Agrin's body, one man, two men, three men, until eleven had gone leaving only Pyris to put his weight on one leg sending it into the still lifeless body beneath him.

This was too much for the native Cornish crowd and they started to surge forward.

Just as this occurred, Agrar broke free and dived over towards Alvaria, grabbing hold of his dagger.

Mayhem ensued for a moment and then Pyris took one final step onto Agrin and as his left leg left the boy's body, Agrar's dagger was only a few inches away from him.

As Agrar was about to thrust the dagger into Pyris, a cough rose into the air from Agrin's body, then another cough and another. Agrar dropped the dagger, stupefied as to what was happening and stood looking down onto his son on the sand below.

Pyris knelt down beside the body.

Agrin was alive, but how could that be? All those millennia ago, before the discovery of artificial respiration and CPR.

Agrar also knelt down and held the boy's body in his arms. He felt cold as he had been submerged for over fifteen minutes but this had helped to preserve his brain cells from dying.

Alvaria spoke. "Husband, remove his clothes, we must make him warm."

As the crowd looked on in amazement at such strange events, Agrin was quickly stripped and wrapped in dry garments to warm his body.

How had Pyris known what to do to save the boy?

***

Long, long ago, Pyris' people, the Caspitarians, were preparing for a mighty battle as a thousand ships waited to receive the order to come ashore and invade their homeland.

Each ship carried a hundred men, making an invading force of one hundred thousand men. The odds looked bad for Pyris and his people for although they could fight and defend their land they were a very peaceful people and not naturally aggressive like so many others who waged war upon them.

As the thousand ships awaited, a huge storm erupted at sea and decimated the invading armada. A few ships escaped but over ninety percent were pulverized by the storm's power and were sent down to the bottom of the sea. Thousands upon thousands of men drowned, many lay on the beach half drowned whilst many others were washed up onto the shore and were too weak to move.

The Caspitarians spotted the body of the captain of the fleet and surrounded his body as it lay on the sand. As an act of insult they marched over him together with many others of the invading force who had drowned.

As a result of this, three men were unintentionally revived by this primitive and crude version of artificial respiration.

Many people drown, but their hearts sometimes still beat even though no breath exists. The marching of men over their bodies had compressed the ribcage and had either helped remove water from the lungs or in the case of dry drowning where the lungs are free from water, they had reactivated the respiratory process.

The Greeks eventually called this 'the walk of life' and from that day they deemed it as a gift from the Gods as it gave mortal men the power of life. It did not always work, in fact, most times it did not, and when this unfortunately was the case it was thought that the drowned person's soul had already been taken by the Gods.

The three men who were unintentionally revived were later executed, a bitter irony after being saved by 'the walk of life'.

This is how Agrin had been saved and now all who were assembled on the beach had truly witnessed a miracle in their time.

**

Agrar stood up and looked around as Alvaria and some of the womenfolk attended the boy who was slowly coming out from a state of unconsciousness. He spoke out to all assembled, both Greek and Cornish. "Who here rescued my son from the sea this day, come forward, I command you?"

Three men stood in front of the chieftain and spoke. "We pulled your son from the sea and laid him down upon the sand, but we did not save him, Agrar."

"What do you mean you did not save him?"

"We took him from the boy they call Stick."

"Surely not," said Agrar. "Are you sure?"

"Yes, Agrar, it was the boy, Stick."

"But how did he know where to find him, he's just a boy and a very strange one at that?"

"It would seem that he knows the tide and undercurrents well as he went to the end of the timber supports and waited in the hope of rescuing your son, Agrin."

Agrar looked over at the stanchions that would support the wooden jetty decking whilst searching with his eyes for the rescuer of his son.

"Where is the boy, Stick!" shouted Agrar.

"He has vanished," said one of the men.

"Organise yourselves into search groups and spread out to find him!" shouted Agrar.

He turned to Pyris and knelt down in front of him. He kissed the Greek's feet and stood up.

"I, Agrar, chieftain of this land, am a strong and feared leader. But it is you, Pyris, and the boy Stick who have saved my son Agrin this day." As he spoke to Pyris he once more wondered why the Gods would make the sea act the way it had, taking Agrin with the intention of claiming his life.

Agrin was carried back to the village by his mother and father and soon the Greeks were back at their labours making the wooden decking ready to erect the next day. As they did so, the Cornishmen were searching in groups for the boy Stick who had, unbeknownst to everyone, run off after swimming ashore. He had not hung around to witness the miracle performed by the Greeks and was convinced that his friend Agrin was dead and as it was he who had dragged him from the sea, he feared the wrath of Agrar who may have blamed him for the drowning of his son.

As the day neared an end, no sign of Stick could be found so the search was abandoned.

Night time fell and the Greeks settled down in their camp upon the beach whilst Agrar spent the evening next to his son, recovering from his near fatal drowning earlier that day.

Agrin lay very weak with a fever now developing.

***

The next day much work was done down on the beach as the decking support timbers were laid. The Greeks were eager to get their ships loaded with tin and return to their homeland of Caspitaria and defend it from the Tantarian attack.

As day elapsed into evening, Agrar and Alvaria kept a vigil beside their son Agrin.

"Oh, husband, perhaps the Gods are angry at my return home and are now punishing us all again through our son," said Alvaria.

"No, I cannot accept this as so, for yesterday as I pissed upon the sea and cursed the Gods, I felt this was not so as during my sleep I saw the ancestors and in my dreams they told me it was not one of our Gods nor one of the Greek Gods who was responsible, but another Demon God from far away, summoned by a man now upon our shores."

Suddenly, Agrin opened his eyes as he lay upon the bed and looked up at where the voices of his mother and father were coming from.

"Agrin, my son," said Agrar. "You are alive and well, may the Gods be praised."

As Agrar looked upon his son, Agrin blinked continuously, the fever had now passed but another problem now arose.

"Father, I have no sight," said Agrin in a frightened voice.

Agrar and Alvaria knelt down beside the boy and Alvaria said, "Worry not, my son, for your fever has now lifted and your body needs time to adjust and heal."

The three embraced and shortly afterwards Agrar left the roundhouse to send a message to Mendax the Dream Teller, summoning him to his home to discuss Agrin's condition.

Agrar spoke to the men of the village. "Fellow Agrarians, what news is there of the boy they call Stick?"

"No sign of the boy can be found anywhere," replied one of the men.

Agrar instructed several of the men to start moving the tin stored in the nearby caves close to the beach and to organise themselves to carry on through the night as the full moon of the evening would give them enough light to do so.

"How is your son, Agrar?" asked one of the men.

"His fever is gone and now he must rest so that his body heals and his strength returns." Agrar continued to say. "If anyone notices anything strange in any man, be they Cornish or Greek, then come directly to me and tell of such things." He did not explain why before returning to his house to await the arrival of Mendax.

CHAPTER 13

During the night, both Cornish and Greeks worked in the bright moonlight that now fell upon the land. The jetty decking was making good progress and a lot of tin was now being taken down to the beach from the nearby caves.

Pyris and Aquilla felt very relieved as now things were really coming together, resulting in an impressive wooden structure stretching way out to sea.

Other jetties had been constructed before on this spot but over the years violent storms had destroyed these man-made structures. This had been very disheartening for the tin traders but was accepted as there was nothing that man could do about it.

The Greeks would pay with goods and bronze objects yet to be seen by the Cornish.

***

Few swords existed in this land three thousand years ago, but now many would be traded for the Cornish tin. This was a sign of the times in the late Bronze Age and was due to a mass migration from many parts of Europe to many parts of this island. Where you had a lot of people is where you would also encounter a lot of trouble. In the early and mid-Bronze Age this island was a peaceful place with land

and lives for all to enjoy and for a time it was a utopia where greed and want did not poison the minds of men.

Nature was in balance with all who lived here and the human spirit was one of goodness to the people who lived in both harmony and fulfilment.

Bronze, a gift of discovery sanctioned by the Gods for man to discover and use for good.

Bronze, the metal of the Gods, copper and tin mixed into this magical alloy and used for over a thousand years by the Agrarians of Cornwall.

Bronze, first used by man to make tools, implements and decorative items and as time went by, it was used as weaponry against his brothers and sisters; and as it was man's wish to destroy, he would be led to discover the metal of death which now became known across the world as iron.

It took many centuries for the transition from bronze to iron and many who lived at this time did not accept this new metal, as bronze was deemed holy by those of a spiritual nature.

Way into the future, such people as the Celts, Romans, Saxons and Vikings would come and although their swords would be made of iron they would still use bronze for decorative items i.e. brooches, clothing pins, clothing fasteners, bracelets, buttons and statues.

A sword from the Bronze Age can lay in the ground for thousands of years and be dug up in good condition and still capable of being used as a weapon, whereas an iron sword will soon decay and rust away in a relatively short time.

Man should have been content with bronze, a gift of discovery from the Gods.

***

Mendax the Dream Teller arrived at the house of Agrar and spoke to the chieftain about his son's condition. "The boy has been through a terrible ordeal, Agrar."

"Yes, and we are blessed that he is here now, safe and sound with us, even though he has at present lost his sight."

"Worry not, Agrar, for although a great power was summoned to take your son into the sea, a far greater power has saved him."

"What sort of power can match the actions of a Demon God?" asked Agrar.

"I will tell you now, my chieftain, and it is something so simple that even a child can do it."

Agrar listened eagerly to the mystic's explanation.

"You see, Agrar, your son was saved by faith and by love."

"But he was pulled out of the water by men who took him from the boy they call Stick."

"I know this Agrar."

"How can you know, for you were not at the beach this day?"

"The boy Stick came to my house this afternoon as he was scared."

"Scared of what?" asked Agrar.

"Scared of you, Agrar."

"But why, Mendax?"

"Because the boy has always been treated as an outcast by all others of our tribe."

Agrar could not argue with this as he usually had no time for the boy and did not like Agrin playing with him.

"The boy is different from most," said Agrar.

"Yes, he is, but he has a heart and a soul just like you and I."

Agrar nodded in agreement with this.

Mendax continued to say, "The only person of our tribe who accepted him and showed him friendship was your own son and this has helped save him from the sea."

"How was this so?"

"The boy, Stick, had faith in saving your son and even endangered his own life by diving into the sea and risking being pulled under by the strong currents."

As Agrin lay close by, both he and his mother were listening to the explanation given by Mendax.

"But the real thing that saved your son was love, as he was Stick's only friend anywhere."

A feeling of shame came over Agrar and he asked as to where Stick now was.

"He is at my home. Or, at least, he was when your men came and summoned me here," replied Mendax.

"Then let us hope he remains there until you return," replied Agrar.

Agrar asked Mendax to bring the boy to his house in the morning and told him to let Stick know that he was grateful to him and wished to thank him in person.

Once Mendax had left the roundhouse, Agrar sat beside his son and told him stories of long ago, stories passed down from generation to generation. As he told his son of the tales and legends of their Agrarian ancestors, a great feeling of compassion was felt by him for the boy Stick.

As he sat beside his son he asked, "Do you feel pain anywhere, son?"

"No, Father, I feel only joy."

"Joy, why is this, Agrin?"

"Now, Father, you have accepted Stick, so I can play with him at any time and with your blessing, is this not so?"

"Yes, my son, it is so."

Agrin's sight had still not returned but everyone was convinced it soon would.

***

Mendax returned to his home where he told Stick he had saved Agrin and that Agrar acknowledged this and wanted to thank him personally the next day.

Tomorrow, the loading jetty would be finished and on the first high tide of the morning, the first ship would be loaded with tin before the hazardous journey of six thousand miles by sea would begin.

How many ships would return safely to Caspitaria?

Did even the Gods know this?

Where had the Demon God who created the giant wave come from and why had he done so?

CHAPTER 14

At first light, all awoke and waited until the tide was right for the first ship to be loaded. A small amount of work still needed to be done to the jetty and was soon started. The tide would take six hours to come in and six hours to go out, therefore, it was agreed that if it were possible, the tin would be loaded at night as well as during the day. The tin had been melted into manageable to carry ingots and was now being loaded onto the first ship. Special care was taken to balance and secure the load, as if rough seas were encountered on the voyage home, the ship may list if the tin moved to one side of the ship due to wave movement.

It was decided that Pyris' pilot ship would remain until the last Greek ship was loaded with tin and ready to leave in about two weeks' time. Pyris was very curious about this new land he had now travelled to and so had spoken to Aquilla when they had both agreed that he would go and explore the area and try to learn as much about the Cornish as he could. He would later in the day speak to Alvaria, asking her to translate his request to Agrar, also asking for a local guide in his quest of discovery.

Pyris was a curious man and wanted to learn as much as he could before sailing home. He was also determined to learn as much of the native language as possible and felt a deep affinity with the land and its people.

***

Agrar had decided several things about the boy Stick and as he was about to leave the roundhouse to wait outside, the silhouette of a boy appeared in the doorway. He beckoned the boy Stick inside, firstly letting him speak to Agrin for a while before he would talk with him.

"Agrin, it is me, Stick."

Agrin held out his hand and searched for Stick's arm which he held tightly. "Stick, you saved me from the sea and I owe you my life for this."

"Well, I'm sure you would have done the same for me, Agrin," came Stick's reply.

"Yes, I would, a thousand times over."

As the boys talked, Agrar and Alvaria sat together on the other side of the roundhouse. They both listened to Agrin and Stick and were impressed with their deep bond of friendship and loyalty to one another.

Alvaria turned her head to face Agrar and said, "How will you reward the boy, husband?"

"I will give him three things, these being firstly, a new home unlike the badly maintained house he lives in. Secondly, I will have the finest spears and axes made to give to him. And thirdly, I will grant him one special wish."

"What do you mean, Agrar, special wish?"

"Whatever the boy needs, wants or desires more than anything in the world I will do it or make it happen."

"Would you even give him your ceremonial gold neck and arm torcs that you treasure so much?"

Without hesitation, Agrar replied, "Yes, even my gold."

Alvaria was most impressed by this decision.

The boys talked for a few more minutes before Agrar and Stick walked outside to where many inquisitive villagers had gathered. They walked into the centre of the village together and Agrar asked Stick what he would like more than anything else in the world. The boy answered, "You mean that whatever I ask for, you will let me have?"

"Yes, my boy, what is it that I can give you here and now in this village amongst all its people?"

Stick smiled, he knew exactly what he wanted and said, "A name."

"You have a name already."

"No, I mean a real name, a tribal name, one of the Agrarian people."

Some of the villagers shouted out derogatory names towards the boy before Agrar intervened and said, "Do not mock him anymore, or you will answer to me. For too long we have treated him as an outcast but now he has proved himself more worthy than any of us by his deeds and actions by saving Agrin from the angry sea."

The villagers quickly dispersed and went about their business, leaving Agrar to figure out a new name for Stick.

"Tell me, Stick, before I give you a tribal name, do you know anything of your past or where you came from?"

"No, my chieftain, I know nothing of such things unlike everyone else here, all I can tell you is that I was abandoned here as a baby by persons unknown."

"Mmm, I will ask Mendax if he can shed some light on this subject and I will give you a name soon, I promise, but until then you will still be known as Stick."

"I can live with that as I have done so all of my life."

"You are free to return to my home and speak with Agrin and are welcome here at any time."

Stick felt good about this as now he had been accepted by Agrar and soon everyone else would treat him as an Agrarian.

Soon, the two boys were once again chatting.

Mendax had come to the village from over the hill and he and Agrar discussed many things, the most important being how to help Agrin regain his sight.

***

Pyris arrived at the village to also speak with Agrar to tell him of his intention to stay for a while and explore this part of Cornwall before returning to Greece. He was taken to the chieftain's house which now had many people inside it. Alvaria translated for the men as they settled down into discussion.

"How is the loading of the first ship going?" asked Agrar.

"Very well," replied Pyris who went on to say, "We will pay you for every ship loaded with tin. Today Aquilla's ship is being loaded and when this is completed, payment of goods will be made to you."

Agrar nodded and asked a servant to bring food and drink for all.

Mendax had noticed something under Stick's left armpit and walked over to him for a closer look. He asked, "What is the marking beneath your arm, Stick?"

Stick raised him arm up for everyone to see.

"It looks like a bird," commented Agrar.

"Yes, it is," agreed Mendax who was examining the tattoo of a raven, instantly recognising this as a marking only given to people known as the Patriarchs of the Stones. "Have you ever wondered about this tattoo before, Stick?" he asked.

"No, I have not, as I have always had it and so have just accepted it as a part of me," replied Stick.

Mendax informed Agrar of the importance of such a tattoo and that Stick must have been connected with the

Patriarchs, Priests and Guardians far to the east at a place known as The Stone Circle of the Salbs who were a race of special people; holy men and women both equal in rank and status who lived at this spiritual centre for Europe three millennia ago.

The modern name for this Stone Circle of the Salbs is Stonehenge, once part of an incredibly advanced race of people brought together on this island for one purpose – to try and interact with the Gods and also to learn through occult practices the meaning of life upon this earth. It was also a place of healing with the surrounding landscape littered with giant roundhouses where people either lived or were healed by the Patriarchs of the Stones. These occult practices would vary incredibly and range from medicines to ancient magic. The Salbs treated women equally and worshipped both male and female Gods and deities, as did the Greeks from where Pyris and the men of his ships had come from.

***

The first ship was now loaded with tin as the loading jetty had been completed. It was decided that two ships at a time, one either side of it, could now be loaded. The first ship was Aquilla's and as he was the captain of the fleet, he would, in the next hour or two, set sail for his homeland of Greece, to Caspitaria, a kingdom unrecorded in any history book as it existed over three thousand years ago. It was a small kingdom but the most beautiful in all of ancient Greece and its surrounding islands.

Agrar, Mendax and Pyris had finished talking and all three men made their way down to the beach to watch Aquilla's ship sail home.

Alvaria stayed with Agrin and Stick inside their house. She looked over at Stick and asked him, "Have you ever wondered about your mother and father, who they are or were?"

Stick replied, "Yes, many times, but I have always come to the same conclusion."

"And what is that, Stick?"

"That I was born a freak."

This shocked Alvaria who went on to say, "Stick, you cannot say that, so please do not think it."

Agrin joined in the conversation, saying, "Stick, I have no sight at the moment which has made me realise a few things."

"What things?" asked Stick

"Well, if everyone in the world went blind they could not judge a person by the way they looked as they could not compare them to anything or anyone else."

Stick thought for a moment before answering. "Then perhaps all men should be blind, avoiding a life of unfair discrimination against others like me."

"Let us not worry about what others think, Stick, because now my father, the mighty Chieftain Agrar, has accepted you as one of us and from now on you will be thought of as an Agrarian by everyone."

"Yes," said Alvaria. "You must look upon us as your family now."

"Do you mean that?" replied Stick,

"Yes, Stick, I do. I know I am not your real mother or that my husband is not your real father but as from now, consider us looking upon you as a son, for without you our own son by birth, Agrin, would be no more."

"Yes," added Agrin, "and look upon me as a brother."

Stick felt like he had never felt before. He now had a sense of belonging and one of family. He had never cried before in his entire life but now the tears rolled down his face as a new set of emotions were kick-started into his life.

CHAPTER 15

It was late afternoon as the first ship laden with tin prepared to set sail. Aquilla the Captain had bid Pyris farewell and the two men had exchanged gold finger rings. This was a custom fuelled by superstition and tradition amongst the Greek seafarers. When the men next met the rings would be returned to their respective owners. Words and prayers were said to the Gods before Aquilla's ship slowly disappeared over the horizon sailing back to the homeland of Caspitaria. Aquilla would be able to tell of Alvaria who had now safely returned home to Cornwall and to her family.

When the tides were next right, two more ships would be loaded with tin.

Agrar and Mendax walked together along the jetty and were impressed by the finished structure now standing proudly from the water below them.

"Mendax, have you any more knowledge or information about the Demon God who was responsible for the wave that took my son into the sea and nearly claimed his life?"

"No, Agrar, I do not, but I have some news of your son, Agrin."

"What news?"

"If his sight does not return by the new month in a few days' time then he must be taken to the Forest of Oaks and must spend a night there alone if his sight is to return."

"How do you know this, Mendax?"

"I was granted a vision in my dreams by the Gods last night."

"But must he stay alone? After all, how can he know where to go or what to do without help?"

Mendax thought for a moment before replying. "The boy must be taken to the forest alone and left, as this is his only choice of regaining his sight."

"What if he is not taken?" asked Agrar.

"As I have said, if his sight does not return by the next month, his only chance is the Forest of Oaks or he will know the dimension of blindness for the rest of his earthly life."

Agrar trusted the wisdom and advice from Mendax as the two men looked into each other's eyes for a few moments before walking back to the sand where many things were happening.

Agrar looked over to where Pyris stood talking to some of his fellow Greeks and asked Mendax "Have you ever wondered what the lands across the sea look like?"

"I have seen them, my chieftain."

"But where and when?"

"In my dreams, Agrar, in my dreams; and what the Greeks have said is true about their enemies having total control of the tin supplies at the eastern end of the middle sea."

"Come Mendax, let us return home for the evening and night."

Agrar signalled to Pyris and they left the beach together with Mendax. As they walked along, Agrar asked, "How is it you look like you do?"

"In what way, Agrar?"

"I remember you from childhood."

"Yes, so what are you saying?"

"You have not aged one day, Mendax, and I remember my father also saying the same many years ago."

"Well then, Agrar, the Death God has truly forgotten about my life and will never claim my soul for delivery into the next world."

Agrar laughed out loud and on the way back to the village, made a detour to the caves which stored the tin ingots. One of the caves was well on the way of having its contents emptied and a big stockpile of tin could now be seen upon the beach.

Once they reached the village, Agrar bid Mendax goodnight and returned to his roundhouse where Agrin and Alvaria were awaiting him.

The boy Stick had left earlier and today was indeed a most joyous one for him as this night he would sleep as never before, at peace with the world and more importantly with himself.

***

Night came as it always does, a time for man to sleep and rest, to dream of love or riches perhaps, a man's dreams can point the way to a happy future or torment him of an unpleasant past.

The Greek camp upon the beach lay quiet as the planet turned its back upon the sun, spinning once a day as it circled the sun.

The fleet, now one ship less, lay calmly in the waters of the bay awaiting their turn for loading.

In the silence of the night, upon one of these ships, stood a man, not a man of Greece or of Cornwall, but a

93

Tantarian who had travelled with the Greeks pretending to be one of them. His orders were at the first chance to destroy as much of the fleet as he could and now he was lighting a torch which he would carry from ship to ship as he set fire to them. His name was Crentarus and it had been his actions that had led to Agrin and the giant wave. He was protected by a Demon God who could control the wind and waves at his beckoning.

Crentarus stood upon the deck of the ship which had brought him to this land and began to set fire to it.

The ships of the fleet were anchored closely together and it did not take him long to set several more ships ablaze. He travelled from ship to ship using a small one-man boat as the ferocity of the flames devoured the timbers of the blazing ships. It did not take long before the roar of flames and crackling of wood woke some of the fleet's skeleton crew. There was nothing to be done that could save the burning ships as each was devoured by fire.

Upon the beach, one of the night sentries was sounding the alarm and soon everyone from the Greek camp watched helplessly as several of their ships burned until they either sank or were left as charred and burnt out remains of ships.

Pyris was an intelligent man and instantly knew the destruction lying before him was by the hand of man.

A total of five ships had been lost and now his mind searched for an answer as to who would have done such a thing. Could they strike again this evening and was it the work of one or several men?

Luckily, Crentarus had fled as he had panicked setting fire to the last ship where he had been spotted by a crew member on board of one of the other ships.

Fire is a violent and fierce entity and Crentarus had taken too much time in his actions whilst setting the ships on fire.

The roar and flickering of flame, together with the cracking of blazing timber had given his actions away. He revelled in his deeds whilst he acted in the role of an arsonist and was now making his way ashore where he would await morning and make plans to observe the results of his actions before heading eastwards.

***

The next morning arrived and a meeting was held by Agrar to discuss the events of the past night. Some of the trade goods had been destroyed but as every ship carried some, it was not a setback in any way.

The next tide had come in and two more Greek ships, one either side of the jetty were now being loaded with tin.

Crentarus had been identified as the arsonist and Pyris was now full of ideas for tracking the traitor down. He asked Agrar, using Alvaria as translator, "Can you lend me your Dog Warrior to track down the traitor Crentarus?"

"Yes, Pyris, I will command him this day to help you track the traitor down together with his two most trusted and loyal dogs."

"Thank you, Agrar, when will you do this?"

"In two or three days' time, once more ships are safely on their way back to Caspitaria."

Pyris explained that it had also been the actions of Crentarus that had summoned a Demon God of wave, wind and water to try and take Agrin's soul.

Mendax approached both Agrar and Pyris.

"Mendax, have you heard of the ships set on fire last night?"

"Yes, Agrar, I have, but I now come to you with more dreams and visions given to me through the night by the guardians of sleep."

"Tell us all you can," said Agrar.

"We have all been instructed to set out heading eastwards."

"Who do you mean, we?"

"I must take the boy Stick to the Patriarchs of the Stone Circle, the ones known as the Salbs. You must take your son Agrin to the Forest of Oaks to be healed by a deity who dwells there whilst Pyris and the Dog Warrior must track down the Tantarian Crentarus before he decides to invoke the powers of his Demon God for evil actions upon our land and people."

Agrar knew that what Mendax had told him must be done and so set about preparing to leave the village in a few days' time.

Four men and two boys would leave the village and head east until a sign or an event would tell them to go their separate ways in pairs. The two dogs chosen by the Dog Warrior were known as Night and Day and would accompany Pyris in his quest to track down Crentarus.

Mendax and Stick would travel way to the east to their destination of Stonehenge.

Agrar would take Agrin to the Forest of a million Oaks but he would have to leave his son there for one night alone or he would never regain his sight.

Men both Greek and Cornish were appointed by Pyris and Agrar to take command whilst they were away.

The day soon passed and it was time for Agrar, Agrin, Mendax, Stick, Pyris and the Dog Warrior to leave. Three separate quests for three very different reasons. Maybe all would succeed, maybe all would fail, what is their destiny, these men and boys of the Bronze Age?

CHAPTER 16

Crentarus had now fled the area and it was time for the men, boys and dogs to start their journey east.

Agrar and Agrin bid Alvaria farewell, "Goodbye, Mother," said the boy as he nestled into her arms for a hug.

"We shall return soon," said Agrar, "and our son will, if it is the will of the Gods, have his sight restored to him."

"Yes, I will" remarked Agrin in a positive and enthusiastic voice.

The group set off following the coast for several miles. As they travelled, Pyris and the Dog Warrior led in front with the two dogs trying to pick up the scent of Crentarus. Pyris had given the Dog Warrior a piece of clothing that had been recovered from the first burnt out ship. It had survived the fire as it had been contained inside a small bronze chest containing Crentarus' belongings and now Night and Day sniffed in their search for him.

Agrar and Mendax followed behind Pyris and the Dog Warrior and at the rear walked Agrin and Stick, hand in hand, like the best of friends do.

"Are you scared, Agrin?" asked Stick.

"No, I am not because I want my sight back so much that I will do anything, so spending just one night in the Forest of Oaks alone seems a simple thing to do. Anyway, most people are scared of things they see or have seen and at the moment normal fear seems to have left me."

"Well, I still think you are brave."

"What about you, Stick? You and Mendax are going to have to travel on foot for weeks before you arrive at the Circle of Stones, are you not the tiniest bit worried about what may happen to you there?"

"No, I am like you."

"In what way?"

"Since my life has changed and your father and the villagers have accepted me, I fear nothing. I am an Agrarian from the far south west so people better watch out or they will answer to me."

Both boys laughed and laughed at Stick's statement.

Eventually, the coastal track came to an end so they all headed inland and followed a river valley which would lead them many miles in the direction of the Forest of a million oaks. Many Bronze Age people lived along river valleys and several roundhouses were passed along the way by Agrar and the others, arousing much curiosity from the inhabitants.

A little further on and towards the end of the valley, a large shadow could be seen upon the ground in front of the travellers. Everyone looked up to see a giant Cornish eagle circling directly over a hill in front of them.

"It is a sign," said Mendax, "and we must now climb to the top of the hill and see what the eagle wants us to see."

Agrar took over from Stick and guided his son up the hill. This was a very difficult thing to do, so Agrar carried Agrin most of the way.

"Is it one of the giant eagles, Father?" asked Agrin.

"Yes, my son, it is and it is circling right above us now," replied Agrar.

The group reached the top of the hill and observed the landscape, looking for anything that may relate to their quests.

"Over there, in the distance to the right," said Agrar as he pointed to what looked like a mighty forest.

"Yes," replied Mendax, "this is where we must part company, Agrar."

Agrar bid everyone good luck as he and Agrin separated from them.

Pyris pointed to the distant forest and spoke but as his vocabulary in the Agrarian language was limited, nobody really understood what he was saying. He had been told of this forest by Alvaria before leaving the village and now he was saying out loud to everyone, "O mighty Zeus, protect this man and his son as they both seek help in the Forest of Oaks."

One of the symbols associated with the Greek God Zeus was the oak tree and Pyris thought it may help Agrar in their time in the forest. Perhaps Zeus himself would help Agrin regain his sight.

Agrar and his son faded away into the distance as the others waited and rested awhile.

The Cornish eagle had disappeared and it would seem that another sign would come when it was time for Pyris and the Dog Warrior to go their separate way from Mendax and Stick.

***

"Father, my legs are getting tired and heavy," said Agrin.

"Worry not, my son, as the entrance to the forest is in my sight. Let me carry you upon my shoulders."

As Agrin travelled on Agrar's strong, broad shoulders, the evening fell upon them and the temperature started to drop as they followed a track deep into the forest.

The oaks stood grandly upright as they had done for centuries and were considered a very holy and spiritual tree, highly revered during the Bronze Age and beyond into the Iron Age by the Celts. The roots of this divinely majestic tree were specially designed by Mother Nature to tap into energies within the ground and with the right knowledge and training these trees could help humans with many problems of mind, body and spirit.

The tree formation started to change into a giant spiral of ten thousand trees. Agrin got down from his father's shoulders which, although strong, now ached.

"Hold onto my hand tightly, Agrin."

"Yes, Father, I will," said the now nervous voice of Agrin who had not really worried up until now about staying in the forest all night alone.

The spacing between the trees was becoming less which greatly reduced the light and as they walked, the spiral of trees became tighter and tighter.

Agrin sensed the tension in his father's hand which he held on to tightly. Suddenly, a large clearing stood in front of them both. They made their way into the middle of the circular space. The moss underfoot lay densely beneath their feet like a luxury carpet.

"Agrin, my son, I must leave you here now."

"I know, Father."

"Do not fear, my son, as I will wait on the outer edge of the forest and will return at first light by which time you will once again be able to see me."

Agrin sat on the soft moss of the clearing, devoid of all sight, alone and not knowing what would happen to him during the night.

As the hours passed to nearly midnight, a warm glow came over Agrin and he lay down and instantly fell asleep.

***

Agrar had been waiting on the edge of the forest and was pacing up and down as he could not relax with the many thoughts and concerns for Agrin racing through his mind. He was now in two minds – one was to stay put as instructed by Mendax and the other was to go back into the forest as far as he dare, keeping out of sight and sound from anyone at the centre where Agrin lay sleeping.

There was just enough moonlight to help him re-enter the forest and as he carried a spear he relaxed a little as he slowly made his way back into the forest. He decided to go as far as the spiral of ten thousand trees which directly encircled his son.

Agrar was typical of Bronze Age man and was very in touch with nature and the earth's natural energies. He felt the power within the forest and decided to sit for a while at the base of an oak tree. This felt good to the chieftain so he closed his eyes and let the feeling he was experiencing take him into a state of peacefulness and contentment. He had only experienced this state of euphoria a few times in his life.

The minutes passed and during this time Agrar was at one with himself and the universe. He opened his eyes and stood up. He looked down to see where his spear was, but could not see it, so he started to search for it but could not find it. He continued to look and as he did so he noticed a strange glowing light moving about the trees at ground level and cautiously made his way towards the mystery object. As he got closer and closer, the figure of a woman could be made out wearing a thin gown of what looked like green light.

Agrar watched and observed, not really knowing what best to do for himself or for Agrin's sake.

He was now very close to her and Agrar could see the strange figure bending over and picking mushrooms in the dark forest night.

So far, he could only see her from behind but she knew he was observing her and stood up straight, still with her back facing Agrar.

There was deadly silence and then Agrar decided to speak to her. "Why do you pick mushrooms in the middle of the night, alone and deep within the forest?"

"And why not, Agrar?" came the reply.

This surprised the chieftain. "Surely," he said, "it would be far easier to pick the mushrooms in the daytime?"

"Not for me," she replied.

"Why is that so and what is your name?"

The mystery woman laughed, her back still facing Agrar. "My name is Faunata."

"Well, Faunata, tell me, why do you pick your mushrooms at night?"

Faunata turned to face Agrar and as she did so she said, "Night or day, they are the same to me."

Agrar let out a gasp of surprise as now she fully faced him and he could clearly see that she had no eyes.

"Were you not told to stay out of the forest if your son was to be given back his sight?"

"Yes, that I was, but like any father I feared for the boy alone all night."

"That was a most foolish mistake, Agrar, as now you must join your son in the dimension of blindness until you both leave this world."

Faunata was a Forest Deity who could do either good or bad magic. She could and would have taken away Agrin's blindness and given him sight once again but Agrar had disobeyed the instructions that Mendax had given him.

"No, Faunata, surely not!" And with that, a bolt of bright blue light was projected into his eyes by her. "May the Gods curse you, Faunata!" yelled Agrar.

"The Gods cannot interfere with me here in my domain, Agrar, and now you must follow my voice to where your son sleeps."

Agrar stumbled and fell several times as he tried to follow Faunata's voice back to where Agrin lay.

"Here, hold onto my gown," said the Deity as they walked.

Soon, Agrar, was reunited with Agrin. Both were now helpless and at the mercy of Faunata.

"Son, I too am blind now."

"But how, Father?"

"I disobeyed the instructions given to me and returned back into the forest as I feared for your safety."

Agrin knew his father had acted out of love for him. As they were speaking, Faunata observed the father and son and said, "In this world, often a choice must be made. This time, Agrar Chieftain of the Agrarian peoples, you made the wrong choice and have paid with your sight. If you had stayed out of the forest, by now you and your son would both have sight. You made a mistake but you are not a bad man, just a victim of consequence as are most men of this world."

Agrar held Agrin's hand and asked the Deity, "I beg forgiveness for this and ask that you help us by restoring our sight."

"This I cannot do, Agrar, only one of the Gods of this land has that power and can do what you ask."

"Then I will call upon him."

"The Gods are forbidden to interfere with the matters of this earthly world and can only influence and guide mankind."

As Agrar meditated beneath the oak tree, his spirit had been fortified with a positive energy within. He dropped to his knees and tilted his head back with his face pointing skywards. "O God of my people, of the Agrarians of whom I am chieftain, I beseech thee and ask for your mercy as I have made a mistake which has now resulted in blindness for both myself and my son."

Agrar felt full of a power which flowed through him as he prayed to the unnamed God of these Cornish tin traders. He now had such a faith and sense of purpose that his intuition drove him like never before.

Agrar stood next to his son and waited and as he did so, Faunata said, "I am sorry to see you grovel and beg like this, Agrar, for it will only lead to disappointment for you until the future day when your spirit will ascend to the home of your ancestors in the sky."

It would appear that Agrar and Agrin would remain blind for the rest of their lives and that nothing could help them as they stood deep within the Forest of Oaks.

***

"Father, we are doomed," said Agrin in a voice full of hopelessness and desperation.

"Hold my hand, son, and wait."

Agrin's hand once more held his father's as the two figures waited in the clearing at the centre of the spiral of ten thousand trees.

Faunata watched and was just about to laugh to herself and leave when suddenly the ground beneath them began to shudder.

Cassitar, God of Tin, stood between Agrar, Agrin and Faunata.

Agrin and his son could not hear the words spoken between the God and the Forest Deity as they communicated, not by language, but by a spirit energy not of this earth.

"Who are you and what is your business here?" asked Faunata.

"I have come to help Agrar and Agrin."

"That you cannot do."

"Why not?"

"Because it is forbidden for any God, if that is what you are, to interfere in human matters."

"Yes, that would normally be the case."

"Then you are a foolish God and will lose any powers you have and be banished by all the other Gods of this land."

Cassitar turned to face Agrar and Agrin and said to Faunata, "It is forbidden for mortal man to lay his eyes upon any God, so as both Agrar and his son are blinded and have asked for my help, it is possible for me to stand here in this form."

"You, Faunata, have made this possible so I thank you, for you have helped Agrar without meaning to."

"But you are still forbidden by the laws of this universe to physically help mortal man in any way."

"Faunata, look at both Agrar and Agrin, look deep inside of them both with your spirit then look at me and tell me of what you notice."

Faunata used her vision of spirit to look at all three and suddenly let out a gasp of surprise. She turned to face Cassitar and said, "They have a part of you in them, but how can that be?"

"I am Cassitar, God of Tin and eight thousand earth years ago I deposited my tin and copper across the far south west of this island." He went on to explain to Faunata

105

that he saw far into the future of this island and of its people who would eventually be known as the Cornish. He felt much love for the land of Cornwall and its people and now at this time, men and women had worked with his tin so much that traces of it existed in their blood. It was only a small, tiny amount but all the same it was there and so by this fact and that that father and son were now blind, Cassitar could now be present to help them both.

"I want you, Faunata, to tell the chieftain and his son that I am here and that I will heal them both and restore their sight." He also instructed her to tell Agrar of his pleasure with the Agrarian people who traded his tin and made good use of it.

"Tell him also that one day the whole world will come here for my tin, but by then bronze, the metal of the Gods, will be long forgotten, replaced with other metals yet to be discovered by mankind."

"How long will your tin last?" asked Faunata.

"Man will dig it from the ground for another three thousand years and then stop, but some will still remain within the ground, waiting until it is needed and mined."

Faunata explained all this to Agrar who found it a very incredible story and hard to believe.

"Now, Faunata," said Cassitar. "Leave us and go about your life in the forest."

"Yes, Cassitar, I will. This night has been a most interesting one for me as it is not every night that one is visited by a Cornish God. With that the Forest Deity vanished. Cassitar took a final look at both Agrar and Agrin before he restored their sight. He decided he would leave them both a gift to remember him by and to remember the special connection between him and them.

Agrar and Agrin stood still, both awaiting the actions of Cassitar. They could not see or hear anything.

Cassitar approached them both and extended his arms straight out in front of him. He positioned his left and right index fingers, almost touching the foreheads of Agrar and Agrin. He smiled to himself and then a blue light arced from him into the father and son; a power not of this world was projected into them both making each of them instantly collapse onto the soft moss beneath them.

A burst of light shot up into the sky as Cassitar left the forest looking like a shooting star and in an instant he was gone.

***

Both Agrar and Agrin lay beside one another for several hours, safe and undisturbed.

As the morning light filtered its way into the forest, the two awoke and slowly opened their eyes.

"Father, Father, I can see once more."

"Yes, my son, and so can I. It would appear Cassitar looked upon us favourably and has now restored our sight." He embraced his son and stood up, the morning light was still very dim but all around them lay a glimmering dusting of tin. Particles as small as dust, each shimmering like a billion tiny lights.

Agrin stood up next to his father and looked around and as he did so his eye caught two objects lying in front of him and his father. "Look, Father, what are they?"

Agrar walked over and bent down. "They are spears, Agrin."

"Spears? But who do they belong to?"

Agrar picked up the larger one and inspected it, saying, "Agrin, they must have been left here for us by Cassitar."

"Do you think so, Father?"

"Yes, look for yourself."

Agrin picked up the other smaller spear and as they both gazed at the spears both were mesmerized by the bronze spearheads attached to the shafts. They could see that they were bronze but both spearheads had an aura about them and they sensed that these were no ordinary spears.

"Father, my spear is the perfect size and weight for me, can we keep them?"

"Yes, Agrin, they are gifts from a God who looks over us and who has brought us wealth with his tin. When we return to the village we will build a shrine to Cassitar, God of the Agrarians. Come, my son, it is time to return to the village and tell all of what has happened this night."

Father and son started to make their way out of the oak spiral and into the outer forest where they would follow the track back into the open countryside.

CHAPTER 17

Mendax, Stick, Pyris and the Dog Warrior had spent the first night of their quests at a small group of roundhouses that were known to Mendax. He had travelled to an area near Stonehenge before, which would now help them on their journey and possibly save them time whilst travelling.

Mendax had dreamt once more of Agrar and Agrin during the night and his dream spirit had seen what had happened to them deep inside the Forest of Oaks. He felt happy that Cassitar had favoured this Cornish land and their people. It had been Mendax who sent them there, so now that Agrar and Agrin were both safe, with their sight fully restored, he was very relieved at this final outcome.

Mendax and the others were eating and drinking before setting out once more on their travels. They were just leaving the small group of houses when Mendax looked up to see the return of the giant Cornish eagle soaring high above them – this was another sign to them all.

"What does this mean?" asked the boy Stick.

"We must follow the bird until it stops and then we must part company with Pyris, the Dog Warrior and his dogs," replied Mendax.

They followed in the direction the eagle led them, two hours passed and then the eagle stopped and started to soar on the thermal air currents with its shadow directly below at a crossroads upon the track they were all following.

When everyone had reached the crossroads, the eagle started to fly north.

"You must follow this road now," said Mendax to the Dog Warrior and Pyris.

Mendax knew the way to Stonehenge and it was still far to the east. He and Stick would carry on alone, an old mystic and a boy with a tattoo under his left armpit.

***

The eagle flew into the distance and now Pyris and the Dog Warrior had to track down the Tantarian saboteur known as Crentarus.

The two dogs, Night and Day, were always out in front searching for the scent of the Tantarian; it might take an hour, a day, maybe a week or not at all, to find him.

Pyris knew his enemies had many Demon Gods at their disposal and was, therefore, very cautious about this fact.

The Demon God helping Crentarus could only use magic on or with water or air, creating wave or wind as he had done when trying to take Agrin away from his earth life. A Demon god would only do such deeds for man on one condition and this was that upon your death he alone would have the rights to your soul and the more souls he gained, the more powerful he would become with his magic in this physical world mankind dwelt in.

Besides the knowledge of the Greeks and the Tantarians that tin could be found in Cornwall, another mission was now underway by Crentarus.

Firstly, he had set fire to the Greek ships which had succeeded in destroying several of them and now he was heading to a specific place where legend said that the good fortune of the Cornish was protected by a golden cup secretly hidden high up on what is known as Bodmin

Moor. This cup protected the Cornish from plague and pestilence and was placed there five hundred years beforehand and had come from Greece.

The Demon God would guide Crentarus to this cup and he would take away any supernatural powers from it, replacing them with a curse for the people of Cornwall to live under.

As Crentarus headed towards Bodmin Moor, Mendax and Stick were heading towards and would cross Dartmoor, which lay across the border between Devon and Cornwall, whose people were very similar in many ways. Neither quarrelled with each other in the days of the Bronze Age.

Agrar and Agrin were making their way back to the village, Agrin could not wait to jump into his mother's arms and tell her of the adventure that he and his father had experienced at the Forest of Oaks. He also wanted to show off his spear to the other children of the village.

***

Pyris could just about communicate with the Dog Warrior who was a fierce looking man and the hairiest person he had ever laid his eyes upon in his entire life. They were just filling their water canteens made of animal skin when one of the dogs ahead started to bark out a message which was instantly recognised by his master.

The two dogs chosen to track down Crentarus were named Night and Day, both were highly trained but as their names implied, one dog was specially trained to track and hunt by night and the other by day.

Day had picked up the scent of Crentarus and would lead both Pyris and the Dog Warrior to him.

They had no idea of the Tantarian's intention to find and destroy the golden cup protecting this land's people and just thought he was running scared. They also did not know of the Demon God helping Crentarus on his mission to wreak havoc and misery to all.

The morning soon passed and many miles were travelled by both Crentarus and his pursuers. The landscape started to change as large outcrops of granite peppered the ground, standing proud and making a statement of their own, defying being hidden underground and letting the world know of their existence.

Smoke rising from fires was becoming more and more visible as Pyris and the Dog Warrior approached Bodmin Moor; this was a place of special importance during the Bronze Age and as they travelled, many things caught the eye and attention of Pyris, his favourite being the stone rows which radiated an energy which even he could sense.

He had not been told that these special stones were positioned into the ground along ley lines, which in ancient times men and animals could sense and feel.

This wonder and magic which nature had supplied then has lost some of its power and awe now, but there are those alive, three thousand years later, who can still feel the power and vibration of the stone rows and circles.

It had been a calm day weather-wise, but the wind was now picking up and instead of blowing in just one direction it was a wind as never felt before by Pyris and the Dog Warrior. It blew into them from all directions and was the work of the Tantarian Demon God.

The two dogs, Day and Night, were spooked and freaked out by this occurrence and sat next to a dry stone wall in a bid to get away from the unnatural gusts now becoming more frequent and strong. Without the help of the two dogs, it would now be impossible to track Crentarus.

Pyris and the Dog Warrior sat down with the dogs and tried to communicate with one another as best they could.

The sky became clouded and the light all around was plunged into one of semi darkness. Pyris reached into his shirt and pulled out a chain which hung around his neck. Upon the chain were amulets of the Gods. He gathered several of them in his hand and prayed silently to them. The Greek Gods of the weather and sky were called the Theoi Ouranioi and were commanded by Zeus and Hera. Aeolus, God of Storms and Helios, the Sun God now listened to Pyris as he prayed to them.

"Well, Helios, what do you make of Pyris and his pleading and praying for us to help him?" said Aeolus.

"We cannot interfere with affairs so far away from Greece."

"But our people of Greece bring tin from this place to help them make weapons to defend themselves against the Tantarians who use Demon Gods to help them."

"That is true, Aeolus. But the Cornish have their own Gods, although very different from us."

"Then, what shall we do for the best?"

The two Gods could not come to an agreement or think of a way they could help and were just deciding to leave the matter well alone when Zeus intervened, saying to them both, "You shall both help Pyris because you are not intervening but are using your powers to correct the storm being created by the Demon God. You are restoring the weather to as it should have been without the interference of this Demon God, who will eventually answer to me."

"Yes, Zeus, you are right in this matter and we will calm the storm which is hindering Pyris and the Dog Warrior."

Aeolus and Helios started to use their divine powers to calm the winds and restore the sunlight.

As this was happening, Pyris looked up at the skies and thanked the wisdom and reverence of the mighty Zeus and his lesser Gods who had helped him.

**

Pyris and the Dog Warrior decided to travel no more this day in pursuit of Crentarus, they would gather food and water to sustain and nourish themselves.

The Dog Warrior would instruct the dog called Night to hunt for food during nightfall and if he returned with any prey it would be cooked for all of them there and then.

Both men were tired by the long trek that day as they had increased their walking pace to that of a march.

Pyris, although a fit man, was not conditioned to walking so far in one day and was soon fast asleep upon the moorland.

The dog called Night went in search of food as the Dog Warrior and his remaining dog also rested but not in such a heavy sleep as Pyris who was now dreaming of both his wife and daughter who he missed so very much. His dream spirit travelled far as he slept and, for a brief moment, touched his loved ones who were so far away in a distant land which now desperately needed the Cornish tin which had started to be transported by ship to them.

Today, another two ships had started to sail back to Greece and tomorrow, another two would set sail on that long voyage home.

CHAPTER 18

Agrar and Agrin were making their way home to the village which was only half a day away. They too slept under the stars this night.

Agrin lay next to his father with both of their new spears ready inches from their hands should they need them in case of danger.

Far into the east, Mendax and Stick had reached the enchanted land known now as Dartmoor. It was similar to Bodmin Moor and covered in megalithic structures, stone rows and circles. In that time, three thousand years ago, Dartmoor was a dense forest, very different from now with its large expanses of space and its tors of granite watching over it since the beginning of time.

This night, a small cave next to one of the tors gave shelter to Mendax and Stick, it would be many weeks before they would return home to the land of Cornwall which all those thousands of years ago was called the Cassiterides by the Greeks, cassiterite being the name given to tin all that time ago. How could the Greeks have known of this land so far away from Greece and its islands?

***

Pyris and the Dog Warrior were awoken early the next morning by the dog called Night who had returned to them with freshly killed meat from its hunting in the surrounding area. A fire was soon alight with the meat cooking above it.

Both Pyris and the Dog Warrior had large appetites and once they had eaten would give the dogs bones to chew on with a little meat still attached.

As Pyris was eating he noticed that the giant eagle had returned and was circling in the sky above a rocky area a few miles away. He drew the Dog Warrior's attention to this and both men soon agreed it was a sign for them to follow and shortly afterwards they were both once more on the hunt for Crentarus who had now found the place where the golden cup lay buried. Who could imagine such a hiding place for this object of status, worth and beauty, made of pure gold, how had it got there and why?

***

Five hundred years before this time, in the middle Bronze Age of 1500BC, a Greek ship had been exploring the outer world in the search for new ideas, peoples, anything which the Greeks, who were the most advanced people in the world, could use in their quest for knowledge and development.

The ship was captained by a man called Carusk and besides the crew of passengers there was a Greek princess known as Verona. She was also a devotee of some of the early Greek Gods, now long forgotten in time. She was of a pure spirit and greatly blessed by these Gods.

The ship had sailed far and wide and was just about to return to Greece when a storm broke out taking the ship out of the control of man.

Verona prayed for the crew and not for herself as the ship was savaged by both wind and wave until it nearly sunk.

As quickly as the storm had come, it went, leaving the ship to drift aimlessly upon the seas until it came aground upon the Cornish coastline on the northern shores.

A few injuries were sustained by the crew and passengers but nobody died as a result of the storm.

The ship was badly damaged and it would take many weeks to repair it. During this time, a small group of five men from the ship went out acting as scouting parties across the area. It was during this time that the crew had learnt that Cornwall was rich in cassiterite (tin).

Where the ship had come aground was quite a remote area and very sparsely populated, but over the weeks of repair to the ship, several of the native Cornishmen helped the Greeks, who welcomed this and afterwards, offered them gifts which the Cornish did not reject, but would take no offer of payment or thanks with material objects.

Princess Verona could sense the power and potential of this land together with its people and so asked the ship's captain if they could stay an extra week or two before returning home to Greece.

Carusk reluctantly agreed to this, only because Verona was a princess and the High Priestess. *It is by chance that we have come here... or is it?* the princess thought to herself. If the storm had not damaged their ship, they would never have landed on Cornish soil and far more importantly they would not have made the discovery of an endless supply of tin which would be traded for over the many centuries to come by both Greeks and Cornishmen.

As the days passed, Verona was convinced destiny had brought her here. She had spent many hours praying to the Gods, trying to find out if this was so, but she knew only too well that even the Gods would rarely answer mankind, if ever.

On the last night of the Greeks' stay, Verona's dream spirit was taken to a place high up upon Bodmin Moor and here she was told that when her earthly life was over, her body was to be returned to Cornwall and buried upon the moor at a place that is today called Rillaton.

With her body was to be placed a sacred cup made of pure gold; a cup that existed in a temple far away in Greece where Verona was Priestess. This cup would bring good fortune to the Cornish as long as it remained buried with Verona's body.

The next day the Greeks sailed home with samples of Cornish tin aboard and so this was how the Greeks discovered Cornwall and also tin three and a half thousand years ago.

Verona and the ship returned back to Greece where maps were made of how to find this land which the Greeks named the Cassiterides.

Fifty years passed before the return of Verona's body, together with the golden cup containing good fortune for the Cornish.

Verona had been queen when she had died and now her body was taken, together with the cup, to Rillaton on Bodmin Moor where she was finally laid to rest in a burial cairn made of stone.

Legend says that one day her spirit will return to this world and she will once more be queen, reincarnated on the earth to rule the mightiest kingdom and empire ever known.

***

Pyris and the Dog Warrior were now approaching below where the giant eagle was circling high above in the sky. They could make out the figure of a man standing on what looked like a pile of rocks and stone. It was the Tantarian spy Crentarus.

He looked to be chanting out words and making signs and symbols with his hands and fingers.

Pyris did not realise that Crentarus was summoning his Demon God to make a wind and turn it into a tornado and this he wanted to be directed right over Queen Verona's burial cairn.

Crentarus was now in the final incantation required for the Demon God to produce such a force of nature.

The Dog Warrior commanded both Day and Night to run ahead and attack Crentarus but the opposite occurred, with both dogs cowering behind him. They had sensed the supernatural and unearthly power being summoned by Crentarus.

An unstoppable whirlwind had manifested itself and was directly above the stone burial chamber of Queen Verona.

The two dogs started to howl as the wind started to make an unearthly screeching sound created by the Demon himself as he merged with the intense rotation of air. Nothing on earth or beyond could destroy this manifestation of evil as it had generated a force field around itself, making it impervious and indestructible from any intervention.

Pyris tried to stand and walk towards it but could not and was knocked off his feet.

He tried to crawl towards it but the power of the wind just pushed him away.

The Dog Warrior watched helplessly and cursed the Demon God together with all Tantarians.

The whirlwind had intensified to full strength and was starting to affect the stone burial chamber beneath it. Several of the smaller rocks upon the top of the cairn were sucked up into the rotating hell wind and sent flying like cannonballs outwards in all directions at a force that would kill any man or beast struck by them.

Pyris and the Dog Warrior lay flat upon the ground as it started to quake; nothing could stop the destruction of the burial cairn and the golden cup protecting the Cornish.

**

Verona had for the most part of her life been a High Priestess at the temple back in Greece where the Gods looked down upon her in great favour. She had served them well and was one of Zeus' most liked mortals ever to have served as High Priestess.

The golden cup in the temple had a power within it and was blessed by all the Greek Gods.

As only a short time was left before the destruction of the burial chamber, a supernatural type of SOS was emitted from the cup and the spirit of Verona.

Pyris and the Dog Warrior lay face down with their eyes closed and their hands covering their ears to cut out the deafening noise all around them. One of the dogs suddenly stood up and tried to make a run for it, away from the ensuing mayhem. As he found his legs and started to run, a rock hit him and tore his body in half. Day was killed instantly, without his master or Pyris knowing.

There are two places where you are safe from a whirlwind or tornado: one is outside of it and far enough away not to be affected and the other is right smack bang in the middle of it where it is still. This is where Crentarus was, in the eye of the storm and in perfect safety. The

Demon God had firstly levitated him off the ground and then produced a whirlwind as powerful as any tornado around him. Nothing could destroy it from outside, not even the power of the Gods, but like all things of the physical dimension and world, it had an Achilles' heel, or weak spot, which had been overlooked.

In the last second before the destruction of the burial cairn, something unexpected by Crentarus and his Demon God was about to happen. High above the whirlwind, looking down upon it, was Zeus holding in his hand a thunderbolt which he could send anywhere in the universe to totally destroy whatever he wished. He simply let go of the thunderbolt in his hand high above the whirlwind. It travelled at the speed of light, unnoticed by Crentarus and his Demon God.

The thunderbolt easily entered into the spinning vortex of air, right at the eye of the storm, where no protection existed for Crentarus.

A power was unleashed; an incredible force contained within the whirlwind.

Crentarus was instantly vaporised and a chain reaction started to take place which within a few seconds, resulted in the whirlwind and its evil creator imploding into nothing.

Zeus had saved the golden cup protecting Cornwall and the lives of Pyris the Greek and the Dog Warrior.

No one would ever know what had happened or of Zeus' intervention which was permitted as the golden cup was Greek and Queen Verona had been a Priestess and devotee of the mighty Zeus.

Pyris removed his hands which had given protection to his ears and hearing. He looked up at the burial cairn and was dumbfounded as to what had happened. The Dog

Warrior lifted his head up and looked around as the two men stood up.

Pyris walked up to look at the slightly damaged burial cairn whilst the Dog Warrior walked over to where his dog Day lay in two halves. As he did so, he was joined by Night who yelped and cried at the body of his dead brother. Both dogs were siblings and were very close to each other, play fighting each day for fun and exercise.

Pyris knelt below the burial cairn, holding the amulets which hung around his neck on a chain. He suspected the Gods or even the mighty Zeus himself had intervened and saved him. He started a prayer of thanks. "O, mighty Zeus and Gods of my family, people and ancestors, I thank thee for saving my life and promise I will always serve you in my heart and soul until death when my spirit will ascend to you for your judgement and divine mercy."

He continued to pray and then replaced some stones which had become dislodged by the whirlwind's destructive power. He looked around the landscape and felt a strong connection with this land of the Cornish. Just as he was about to walk back to the Dog Warrior, he heard a female voice behind him. He turned and saw a vision of Queen Verona.

"Fear not, Pyris," she said in such a voice that Pyris was instantly transfixed upon the apparition of her. He could not speak or think as she told him of his family.

"Pyris, your wife and daughter are both well and have my protection from now on; they will never be harmed by your enemies the Tantarians or anyone else. You will return to Greece with your ships of tin and defeat the Tantarians before the end of winter."

On his travels, Pyris had often wondered if he would ever see his family again. Verona could sense this and so appeared to him at this time to reassure him about his worst fears.

Pyris suddenly felt faint and dropped to his knees, he shook his head and rubbed his eyes, moments later he re-opened them to see that Queen Verona had vanished into the ether.

He knew in his heart that the Gods must have saved him and must approve of his mission to return to Greece with the Cornish tin and be reunited with his wife and family.

He slowly made his way back down the hill to where the Dog Warrior had just finished burying his dog. He had been facing the other way so had not seen the vision of Verona or of Pyris praying.

The two men together with one dog now had to return to Agrar's village, where they would tell all of what had happened to them high up on Bodmin Moor where the traitor and spy Crentarus had tried to take away the good fortune and future of the Cornish.

***

As Pyris and the Dog Warrior started to make their way back to the village, Agrar and Agrin's journey home was nearly over. This now left Mendax and the boy Stick to cross Dartmoor and travel on to Stonehenge in the hope of solving the mystery of the tattoo underneath the boy's armpit. What could it mean and what significance would it have once the two reached the place of the giant stone circle?

CHAPTER 19

"What is this place?" asked Stick inquisitively.

"It is the moor of hidden magic (Dartmoor)."

"Why hidden magic?"

"Because it possesses a magic of its own and not one that man can conjure up or make," replied Mendax.

"And what of your magic, Mendax? Have you always had the ability of telling the meanings of dreams and of seeing beyond our world?"

"Yes, my boy, I have, and it is something that makes us both have a connection in life."

"What do you mean, please explain?"

"You see Stick, when I was a boy growing up I knew things and sensed things that no one else did and for this I was treated by some as an outcast, just as you have been treated for being slightly different than others."

Stick knew only too well what Mendax meant as he explained this and nodded to him as he acknowledged this fact about them both. He felt a shared experience in life with Mendax which made him instantly like and accept the old man.

"Were you of Agrarian birth or an outsider like me?" asked Stick.

"I am outsider like you, Stick, but now after all these years I consider myself an Agrarian and am treated that way by all."

"That has now happened to me, Mendax, for my part in the saving of my best friend Agrin, son of the mighty chieftain Agrar."

"Yes that is now so, my boy, as I knew it would be some day."

Stick did not question this as he knew Mendax was indeed a man of good magic, medicine and mystery, but he asked one final question.

"Will Agrin and I always be good friends?"

"Yes, of that you can be sure and you will both have many adventures together on your way through life's mysterious path."

The two travellers settled down for the night on the edge of a wood, they made a fire and spoke of many things, past, present and future. To an outsider they would almost seem like father and son engrossed in conversation about life.

As the fire started to fade, so too Stick drifted off to sleep, followed shortly by Mendax who was not so much asleep but in a trance-like state as he meditated upon life.

***

Pyris and the Dog Warrior had settled down for the night at a small settlement on their way back to Agrar's village where now he and his son had reached home and were sleeping in their own beds.

During the daytime, two more ships had sailed back to Greece, loaded with Cornish tin.

The Greeks and Cornish were getting along together very well and despite the language barrier between them, many friendships were being forged.

The ancient Gods of Greece and Cornwall would do everything they could to help all of the ships return safely, their main powers were ones of nature, which mainly involved the weather.

Aquilla had left days ago and was making good speed towards home as the Gods of wind were making this possible by supplying a full sail of wind at all times. The Greek crew aboard his ship had never known of such luck when sailing before and all felt reassured and pleased that this was now so.

***

"Are you awake, boy?" asked Mendax.

"Yes, I am," came the answer.

"I have heard that you never eat food and that you only drink, is this so?"

"Yes, it is so."

"May I ask you why this is so?"

"If I eat any solid or part solid food then within half an hour I am sick and feel unwell for hours after."

"So, you only drink. But surely a person cannot survive this way all of their life?"

"Well, I am only a boy and do not expect to reach adulthood."

This statement shocked Mendax, especially as the boy Stick had said it in such a way that he expected to die in the near future.

"When we return to the village I will try and help you with my knowledge and medicines."

"Thank you, but you will fail."

"Can you eat anything at all?" asked Mendax.

"A few berries and, if I chew them for enough time with lots of spit, I can eat some nuts."

"Can you tell me anything else about yourself, boy?"

Stick held out his arms towards Mendax and said, "Only that I have the hands and feet of a giant."

The two of them laughed at this fact.

"Come, let us gather our things and continue our travels across the moor."

Mendax always wore a cloak come summertime or winter, whereas Stick wore very little during the summer months and dressed in a top which resembled a modern sleeveless vest. He also wore an early style of kilt and upon his feet he wore sandals and carried a small shoulder bag with him containing a spare pair. Depending upon the type of terrain underfoot it was very important to have the right footwear.

Both Mendax and Stick carried no weapons with them although Mendax carried a crook which he could use as a weapon if needed.

The two travellers, although very different in age and character, found it easy to talk about anything on their journey. Both of their lives were partly shrouded in mystery and secrecy; both were enigmas.

They had been following a row of standing stones for half a mile and had reached one of the moor's highest tors which overlooked a Devon tin mining community known to Mendax. He had decided to come this way and pass through the village, telling all of the Greeks' visit to Agrar's village. He knew one or two of the inhabitants and as he had not travelled this way for some years, he wanted to say hello and to see what new developments had taken place.

As the village came into view, Mendax let out a gasp of disbelief, as below him where the village lay next to a stream where gold could be found, he saw the smouldering remains of all the houses and other buildings. He rushed down to the desolation followed by Stick and as he did so, the real horror manifested itself to him in the form of dead animals and people.

He stood shaking his head in disbelief whilst looking around.

"What has happened here?" asked Stick.

"That I cannot tell at the moment but something terrible has occurred here which should not have."

As Mendax and Stick wandered through the carnage and destruction they had both noticed that several of the bodies had been decapitated with no signs of the heads.

Mendax was relieved to see that only adult bodies lay around and wondered what had become of the children. Perhaps they were safe and in hiding? Pigs and dogs had also been slain, but by who and why?

Mendax made his way over towards the stream, determined to find out what had happened. Stick followed and sat on a large rock a little way from Mendax, whom he wanted to observe.

Mendax knelt down and removed his cloak and bent over until his face was almost touching the stream. He pushed his arms into the water whilst chanting a few words in a tongue Stick did not recognise.

The stream appeared to slow down its flow which made Stick blink several times in disbelief.

Mendax appeared to be talking into the water and to Stick it appeared that the flow of the stream had almost stopped.

Stick decided to close his eyes until Mendax had finished what he was doing. To Stick, magic was something he wanted nothing at all to do with.

Although Mendax's face was almost touching the now still water, an echo could be heard and as he spoke, his words resonated around the settlement.

Stick kept his eyes tightly closed until a few minutes later, when all was quiet and Stick could once more hear the stream flowing on its way towards the River Dart.

"Are you asleep, my boy?" asked Mendax.

"No, just unsure about magic," replied Stick.

"Don't worry about that, Stick. There is much to think about that the stream has told me about the fate of these people and their village."

"Why, what has happened here Mendax?"

Mendax told the boy of what he had seen. "I cannot believe the people of the Stone Circles called The Salbs would do this, but it has been told to me and must be true."

"But that is where we are travelling to, Mendax."

"Yes, I know, but it would appear that a new people rule this island and the old patriarchs, men of spirit and soul, have been replaced by ruthless greedy people who have overthrown the old ways."

"Who are these people who have replaced the true Salb race?"

"They call themselves the Kelanti."

A loud screech suddenly rang out high in the sky, making them both look up to see the giant Cornish eagle soaring above an area of shrubland and bushes.

"What does it mean, Mendax?"

"Let us go and see where the eagle's shadow falls upon the ground and hope there is a reason for this, or if there are any answers to help us decide what to do next."

They both started to climb up towards where the eagle's shadow danced upon the ground.

"What are we looking for?" asked Stick.

"Even I do not know, but this is where the eagle has guided us, my boy."

The two stood still and waited and as they did so the giant eagle disappeared as quickly as it had appeared. A faint noise could be heard coming from within some bushes.

"I hear crying," said Stick.

"Yes, you are right," replied Mendax who called out to whoever was hiding there.

"Hello, can we help you in any way?" he spoke in a soft, reassuring way. He waited a few minutes before repeating his words. A few more minutes passed and just as Mendax and Stick were about to try something else, there came movement from within the bushes.

"Someone or something is moving this way from out of the bushes," commented Stick.

Mendax looked at him and nodded. They both took a few steps back in anticipation of what was coming their way. The movement became more and more until out of the bushes walked a young girl who was seemingly in a state of shock and bewilderment. She looked straight ahead and did not acknowledge the presence of either Stick or Mendax.

"Why does she stare so strangely?" asked Agrin.

"It is because she is in shock and I fear she has seen terrible things happen here at the village."

"Can we help her, Mendax?" asked Stick.

"We can but try, my boy," came the reply.

They both approached her slowly and quietly and smiled to show they meant her no harm. Mendax undid his cape and wrapped it around the young girl's shoulders. Her crying becoming just a whimper. He extended his right arm out to the girl who looked at him before responding by reaching out to him and holding his hand.

The three figures slowly made their way back down to the settlement where they took the girl into a roundhouse and made her feel as comfortable as they could.

The roundhouse gave shade from the mid-summer heat and glare; it was dark, cool and comfortable.

The girl sat upright upon the bed but after a while lay down upon it, falling into a deep restful sleep.

"What has happened to her?" asked Stick.

"I think this girl saw what happened here and fled for her safety to where we found her."

"Then she may have seen her own family killed here?" replied Stick.

"Yes, I fear so. Come, let us look around the settlement some more. We will let the girl sleep as she is safe now."

Mendax and Stick had a closer look around the settlement and decided to put the bodies together and cremate them. This took some time to do but was a task which had to be done, as if the bodies were left they would rot and it would be disrespectful to the souls now departed from this world. Soon the funeral pyre was ablaze with the bodies upon it engulfed by the flames.

It was late afternoon and both Mendax and Stick returned to inside the roundhouse where the young girl still lay sleeping. Soon, they also entered the dimension of sleep and rested peacefully for about an hour before being disturbed by screams coming from the young girl.

Mendax walked over and stood next to her, placing his right hand upon the girl's forehead. He closed his eyes and once more spoke in a tongue not of this land or world. The screams gradually stopped and the girl slowly awoke. She looked at Mendax and asked, "Who are you and what do you want?"

"My name is Mendax and his name is Stick."

"Stick? What sort of name is that?" replied the girl.

Stick half smiled at the comment which in his lifetime he had heard many times before.

"Can you tell me your name?" asked Mendax.

"I am called Amapra."

"If you feel up to it, can you tell us what has happened here, Amapra?"

"Men came from the east, some on horses, they killed everyone including my mother and father. They also took away the children, including my brother."

"Oh, I see," replied Mendax as Stick looked on with a face filled with horror at what she was describing to them.

***

The ruling patriarchs of Britain known as the Salbs had been overthrown after over a thousand years of ruling. These men were spiritual men but were also astronomers, healers and overlords to the whole of southern Britain.

Agrar and his people were known to them but contact rarely occurred between them.

Over the past few years, many people from northern Europe had come to settle in Britain, they had formed an alliance and decided to form an army and overthrow the ruling patriarchs of Stonehenge. Many were killed whilst many others fled to the far corners of this nation where they hid and did not reveal their identities to anyone as they feared for their lives.

The old order of the Salbs had been replaced by a warlike people, intent on cashing in on the country's rich resources.

These new men, motivated by greed and avarice, were known as the Kelanti. They did not respect the old ways and now controlled the rich amber deposits situated to the south east of Britain. The Kelanti had travelled west to Devon to instil fear into the hearts of its men who mined and traded their copper and tin. They demanded all their possessions of value and worth, especially gold – the Kelanti loved gold.

They had taken Amapra's brother and all the other children from this community together with others to use as slaves and to indoctrinate their young minds into the ways of the Kelanti.

Amapra told Mendax she had overheard some of the Kelanti saying that soon a mighty army numbering many thousands of men would come and take the wealth of Cornwall away and control its tin trade, making profit from those forced to work for them.

During the Bronze Age, an army numbering thousands of men was unheard of in Britain, the Kelanti were hiring mercenaries from other parts of Europe, offering wealth and riches to all who followed them.

"What is an army?" asked Stick.

"An army is a group of men who are trained to fight wherever and for whatever their leaders – in this case the Kelanti – command."

"But what do these men normally do when not fighting?"

Mendax laughed and said, "This army of men know and do only one thing, my boy, and that is to kill."

Stick was a little surprised by this answer.

The leader of Kelanti army was called Vorgus and he loathed the people of this land.

CHAPTER 20

Another two ships loaded with tin, again set sail for Greece this day.

Agrar and Agrin had told the people of the village and surrounding area of their mysterious adventure in the Forest of Oaks where they had met the Deity Faunata.

Even the Greek mariners came to listen to this amazing story which was translated and told to them by Alvaria.

Pyris and the Dog Warrior had just arrived safely back at the village and would soon tell of their amazing adventure and the demise of the Tantarian Crentarus and his Demon God.

Agrin had asked his father if he could train him to fight on sand as he could.

"Yes, son, later today we shall go down to the beach and I will show you some basic moves to get you started, is that okay?"

"Oh, yes, Father, I would like that."

Agrar knew their spears were no ordinary ones so he made sure they were not left lying around for people to see. He also instructed Agrin to tell no one of their whereabouts which only they knew about.

Alvaria was getting back to normal life and routine at the village. All those years away from her husband and son now seemed like a fleeting memory.

Agrin walked up to his mother in an excited way, telling her of his ambition to be a great sand fighter like his father.

"You know, my son, fighting is not something to be proud of."

"What do you mean, Mother?" asked the boy.

"There are other things which are more fulfilling in life."

"I know, Mother," said a now rather deflated Agrin.

Whilst a captive for almost six years, Alvaria had seen much sadness and destruction in her life and she did not want her only son to grow up thinking that fighting was so important but as Agrin was just a boy, she would have a very hard job in doing this.

Agrin looked deeply into his mother's eyes and said "Do you think Stick is safe?"

"Oh, yes my son, I feel he is and don't forget he is with Mendax who knows of many things which will help them both on their journey to the place of the Stone Circles."

"Do they have stone circles in Greece, Mother?"

"I did not see any, Agrin but that does not mean there are none."

"Are there boys like me there?"

"Yes, Agrin, there are boys like you there and with your spirit having ambitions to fight."

"Mother, it is not so much as to fight but to learn how to fight."

"What do you mean, my son?"

"I never want to hurt another person but I do need to protect not only myself, but as I grow into a man, to protect others weaker than myself."

"Does that include me, Agrin?" asked Alvaria.

"Yes, Mother, it does, for when I am a man you and my father will be older and may need me to protect you one day."

Alvaria laughed at this as did Agrin. She knelt down and embraced him, both mother and son feeling the flow of eternal love between them both.

***

The afternoon soon came and together Agrar and his son walked down to the beach where men waited for the tide to change so two more ships could tie up to the jetty and be loaded with tin. Some children followed close behind the father and son as Agrin had told them of his wish to learn how to fight upon the sand.

"Well, my son," said Agrar. "I will teach you some tricks first which can help you gain an advantage even before you are forced to fight."

"Tricks, Father, what sort of tricks?"

Agrar began to teach Agrin all he knew about combat on the sand on which he had a reputation of being unbeatable.

"Look up, way above my head, Agrin and tell me what you see."

Agrin looked up into the clear afternoon sky and said, "I see the sun, Father but cannot look at it directly as its power will blind me."

"Yes, my son, and this is your first lesson."

"But Father, I already know not to look into the sun."

Agrar laughed loudly and explained to the boy the lesson he wanted to teach his son.

"If you ever fight on a day such as this, especially in winter when the sun is low, then always try to have the sun behind you, that way your opponent may have the sun's light in his face. He may have to squint as you did which puts tension in the muscles within the head. This can make your opponent slightly slower than you."

Agrin thought for a moment and immediately understood what his father was telling him.

"Tell me more Father, please."

"What would you do if you had to fight more than one man?"

Again Agrin thought for a moment before saying, "That's easy, Father, I would get you to help me fight them."

Once again, Agrar let out a loud belly laugh. "Well, let's just say you are alone and have to fight two men, my son."

He started to give Agrin a practical demonstration by getting two of the men from the beach to simulate an attack on him and as he did so, many people gathered around to see what the mighty chieftain was doing.

As the two men came towards him, he moved to one side so they were now in line with him, putting him in a position of being able to fight one man as the other one was the other side of Agrar's attacker.

"I see, Father, you are trying to use the man you are fighting as a shield, thus stopping the other attacker getting to you," said Agrin.

"Yes, my son, and this can work sometimes with three opponents so always try and use whoever you are fighting as a shield by getting them between you and other possible attackers."

The crowd clapped at this very simple but logical approach to a multiple attack. Some of the village children moved to one side and started to play fight upon the golden Cornish sand, using the strategy Agrar had told his son.

"So, Agrin, think about what I have just told you, for one day it may be of great advantage to you."

Two of the Greeks stepped forward towards Agrar; they thought themselves pretty good as fighters. One was a puncher and kicker, the other liked to wrestle and grapple.

Agrar did not know of this but agreed to fight them one at a time and as the three men prepared for combat, albeit all for fun and demonstration of their skills. The other Greek mariners upon the beach were betting amongst themselves as to who they thought would be the victor.

The first fight began and was between Agrar and the Greek boxer who came at the chieftain with some ferocity and with a ratio of about four punches to every kick. Agrar appeared to move more freely than the Greek, easily avoiding the strikes launched upon him, his reputation was at stake which made the Greek try his best to beat him but the harder he tried the easier Agrar seemed to move swiftly in defence.

"Go on, Father, hit him!" shouted Agrin but Agrar was letting the young, overzealous Greek tire himself out before retaliating. He waited until experience and intuition told him to strike which he did at the speed of light, using a left jab to the chin of the Greek followed by a right uppercut into the lower ribcage as he stepped towards his opponent. The Greek dropped down to one knee and held his hand out with the palm facing Agrar.

Agrin and some of the villagers cheered as the Greek spectators looked on with disappointment on their faces.

Now it was time for the wrestler to see if he could beat Agrar upon his native sand. The fight was started in the traditional Agrarian way of both fighters standing back to back until a horn was blown. You would then have the choice of immediately turning and fighting or quickly taking a few steps forward and turning in preparation for combat.

As the horn sounded, the Greek instantly spun around as Agrar leapt forward, taking two steps before turning round. The Greek was fast and charged at Agrar, his arms outstretched to the sides making a large contact area if he caught Agrar within his charge. The speed of the Greek caught Agrar by surprise as the Greek wrapped his arms tightly around the chieftain. He tightened his vice-like bear hug around him and was just about to play dirty with a head butt when unexpectedly Agrar's right knee launched itself into his groin in which a sickening pain was quickly felt by the Greek due to his testicles momentarily being crushed.

Both men separated and as the Greek lay upon the sand waiting for the pain and discomfort to cease, Agrar stood a few paces away and waited for him to recover.

The Greek eventually stood up and both men began to size each other up for the next move. They put out their slightly bent arms in front of them and approached one another in a cautious manner. Agrar's opponent was a much heavier man than he and so Agrar did not want to be taken down to the floor unless he could retaliate whilst doing so. He put his left arm behind his back which made the Greek wonder why, as did the onlookers.

The Greek got closer and closer and just as he reached and grabbed Agrar's other arm, the chieftain crouched down a little and suddenly jumped up into the air and in a moment was on the Greek's back, with his opponent's right arm held around his own neck by Agrar.

The Greek spun around a few times as he tried to throw Agrar off but he could not do this and so decided to fall backwards and slam Agrar into the sand.

A moment before he planned to do this, which Agrar had already anticipated and wanted him to do, the chieftain dug one of his heels into a nerve within the Greek's leg to which the leg gave way sending him forward face down into the sand with Agrar still having control of him upon his back.

As the Greek hit the sand, Agrar immediately re-positioned himself, putting the Greek into an arm and leg lock to which the Greek tapped down hard upon the sand with his free hand indicating submission, making Agrar immediately release his hold and stand up.

As this happened, the crowd cheered and the Greek onlookers walked away in bitter disappointment.

The Greek wrestler stood up, shook hands with Agrar and followed his fellow countrymen back over to their beach camp.

Agrin ran over to his father shouting, "Well done, Father, you are the greatest chieftain ever of this island."

"Come, my son, let us sit down at the water's edge and I will tell you more secrets of how to fight upon the sand."

Father and son wandered down to the sea and sat, the waves lapping gently over their feet.

"Will I ever be as good as you, Father?"

"I have no doubt of that, my son," replied Agrar who continued to explain a few more aspects on the way he had fought today and in the past.

The first fight between Agrar and the Greek boxer was one involving strikes, kicks and punches and Agrin had wondered how his father's whole body had moved more quickly and smoothly than the Greek fighter.

Agrar explained how this had been possible. "Listen closely to what I have to say, my son, as it is one of the secret ways to help you win in combat."

"Yes, Father, I'm listening."

"When you fight a man whilst standing and you have to move more quickly using a strategy of avoidance, be it leaping, jumping or running, you must breathe high up in the chest."

"Why is this so, Father?" asked Agrin.

"It will give you more spring and lightness of body, only a small amount, but it can only be to your advantage in a fight which chooses strikes."

Agrar stood up and showed his son a demonstration of this breathing technique and how to use it. He told him he must practice this each day from now but only for a few minutes.

"What about the other fight, Father, where you grappled?"

Agrar started to tell his son and demonstrate the next lesson.

"If I am to fight and grapple whilst standing then I must breathe deeply but from my stomach and with my legs bent at the knees more than they are normally bent. This will make you more stable and harder to move by an opponent."

"How does this work, Father?" asked Agrin.

"I do not know, my son, but the ancestors believe that because you are closer to the ground than normal when doing this, you borrow its force and power which gives you more stability."

Agrar told his son to also practice this technique daily but in the order of chest breathing first thing in the morning and abdominal breathing in the evening.

"Do you understand all I have told you this day, my son?"

"Yes, Father, I do, and I will try to practice each day."

"Try, my son, no – you must do it or your ability to fight upon the sand will not be as good as it could be."

"When can I learn the moves to fight men, Father?"

"Soon, my son, but first think about this day and what you have witnessed."

"Yes, Father, I promise I will."

"Come, Agrin, let us go and see how the loading of our tin aboard the Greek ships is going."

Father and son walked over the loading jetty and watched for a while.

"Would you like to go to where the Greeks live, Father?" asked Agrin.

"They are an interesting people, my son, with much to teach us, of this I am sure."

"What about their Gods, Father?"

"We have our own Gods, my son."

"Yes, and I think it was the God of our tribe who helped us in the Forest of Oaks."

"Yes, I too think this, my son, and I also feel it within my heart and soul."

CHAPTER 21

Mendax, Stick and Amapra were heading towards the south coast where Amapra's uncle and aunt lived at a coastal settlement. She had told Mendax that he and Stick could be taken home by boat which would be much faster and safer than on foot. Time was of the essence as the Kelanti would soon push deep into Cornwall and seize the wealth of the Agrarians. It would appear an impossible mission to prepare for and stop so many men trained to kill anyone they came across.

As they travelled south, Stick walked next to Amapra whilst Mendax led the way several paces in front.

"Why are you so thin?" asked Amapra.

"I cannot eat food in the way you and others do as it makes me sick."

"Oh, I see," replied Amapra.

"Will your uncle and aunt let you live with them?"

"I hope so, at least until the Kelanti have gone from this area and then maybe I will return to my home."

"What about your brother?" asked Stick.

"I do not know if I will ever set eyes upon him again as now he is far away to the east where they take all of the captive children to indoctrinate and brainwash them into their ways, making them accept they are slaves to the Kelanti race."

"Maybe one day when my best friend Agrin is chieftain we will go and find your brother and teach the Kelanti a lesson they will not forget."

"To do that Stick, you and your friend would have to grow up into men like them and that I would not like to see. The Kelanti take what they like from whom they want and kill as if it means nothing."

"Then I will one day try and help you find him in some other way," said Stick as his mind tried to think of how to ever achieve this.

The three travellers rested for a while next to a stream where Stick asked the mystic Mendax questions relating as to what was happening in Britain at that time.

"Why do men come here, Mendax, who try to change how we live in this land?" asked Stick.

Mendax suddenly asked Stick and Amapra to remain quiet and still as he wished to ask the ancient spirit of water questions about the Kelanti. He removed his cape and took off his sandals and began walking up and down an area lying parallel with the stream before stepping into it whilst uttering words only known to him.

Stick and Amapra watched in anticipation and as they did so Amapra's left hand reached over to Stick and held his hand.

Mendax adopted a posture in the stream which looked like a press-up position. He chanted more words and lowered himself into the water which covered his entire body. He remained submerged for twenty seconds before he pushed his body up and out of the stream and started chanting more words and re-entered the water.

A mist formed along the stream and as Stick and Amapra observed it, they became slightly scared and unsure so they both decided to close their eyes. They had noticed shapes forming within the mist which now hung above the entire length of the stream, stretching for miles in both directions.

As Mendax merged with the water spirits and lay submerged, many visions came to him. He saw the evil leader of the Kelanti whose name was Vorgus and how the world was now changing. Men had used bronze for over a thousand years as tools and implements but a new race of Kelanti were using bronze to make weapons.

There were no armies on this island and it was a relatively peaceful society, but now Vorgus and his army of mercenaries could go anywhere in the land and take what they wanted. This had angered the Gods, as bronze was a gift of discovery given to man thousands of years ago by them.

After this vision, another one came to Mendax and was one of incredible power which held Mendax under the water for a longer time than normal. The vision was of the boy Stick who sat just yards away from him. It revealed where Stick had come from and why he had the tattoo of a raven under his left armpit which he received when he was a baby and only a few months old.

The visions had revealed many things to Mendax, all of which he could not immediately tell to others.

He had been submerged under the stream for many minutes and his body desperately needed to take breath. He suddenly stood up out of the water and clung to the grass bank next to him as he gasped for air.

Stick and Amapra opened their eyes and ran over to him, both relieved the strange mist had disappeared.

"Mendax, are you all right?" asked the boy.

Mendax looked up and nodded as he lay with his top half against the grass bank and his legs and feet still submerged.

It was another sunny day with a warm breeze flowing through the air; this would soon help dry him off as he clambered out of the stream with the help of Stick and Amapra each pulling an arm in their efforts to help him.

Once Mendax had caught his breath he walked around with his arms outstretched trying to get dry as soon as he could. Once dry and dressed, it was time for the three to set off again. Stick had many questions for the mystic who told him he had learnt much and would reveal all at the right time and in the right place.

***

By evening, the three travellers had reached the coastal settlement on the south west Devon coastline. Here, Amapra told her uncle, aunt and others of the horror she had experienced and seen with her own eyes. These peaceful people now feared for themselves and their families so Mendax tried to dispel these fears by saying, "Good people of Devon, do not fear attack from Vorgus and his mercenaries."

"Why shouldn't we?" asked one of the people now gathered.

"Because the Kelanti are after great wealth of which I assume you have none."

"No, that is true," commented Amapra's uncle who continued to say "Half of us are fishermen and half farmers."

"Then you should be safe," repeated Mendax.

Arrangements were made for a boat to take Mendax and Stick back to the village where they would warn Agrar of the impending danger to his people. The boat would leave at first light the next day and sail west following the coastline from Devon to Cornwall and then further west to home.

During the evening, Mendax spoke with the men about many things whilst Stick sat for hours talking to Amapra.

"Will I ever see you again, Stick?" she asked.

"Why do you ask?"

"Because I like you and you are different than most boys and people I know."

Stick thought she was either mocking or pitying him and so said to her, "I cannot help the way I look and have always wondered what it would be like to be normal."

Amapra smiled, "No, Stick you have it all wrong. You see, I like you just the way you are."

"You do?"

"Oh yes, so please don't change," said Amapra.

This made Stick smile as well.

"I like you also, Amapra, and will one day return here and find you or if you have moved on to live somewhere else, I will search until I find you there."

"Do you promise, Stick?"

"Yes, I do."

Amapra had seen many good qualities in Stick, he was funny looking, yes, but she had sensed his spirit and liked his character very much.

Destiny would play its part one day, for far into the future they would both meet once more.

***

An army numbering many hundreds of men was waiting in Devon for the main body of Kelanti mercenaries to arrive from many parts of the south east. Vorgus, their leader, had promised great wealth for their loyalty and allegiance to him. His intention was to take over all the tin and copper deposits of Devon and Cornwall and make slaves of the people he did not kill. He was a vicious man and would instil instant fear into people by butchering many innocent lives for all to see on his arrival at villages and settlements.

The ancient order of the Salbs whose capital had been Stonehenge and its surrounding area, had been decimated almost to the point of extinction by Vorgus. He had made sure the ruling family would all die without mercy and the patriarchs of Stonehenge known as the Keepers of all Knowledge would die next. Eventually, everyone else connected with them would be either beaten, tortured or killed.

Vorgus knew that a small amount of them would get away and go into hiding but he also knew that they would never speak of what had happened lest they one day be tracked down or be betrayed by others in their new lives, thus giving away their true identity.

***

Mendax and Stick bid goodbye to Amapra and her relatives and boarded a boat crewed by two of her uncle's most trusted friends. As the boat made its way out to deeper water, Stick and Amapra waved to one another, each feeling slightly sad by their separation.

The boat had soon been rowed out to sea and the small sail filled with air pushed it towards the south west, to the home of the Agrarian people.

Mendax and Stick spoke little as they travelled home. Stick's mind was full of thoughts for Amapra whilst Mendax had many plans to make in his mind as he knew only too well that Agrar and his people were now facing imminent extermination by the Kelanti whose army was at this very moment increasing in number by the hour.

The boat passed by the mouth of the River Tamar which separates Devon from Cornwall and was soon hugging the Cornish coastline whilst homeward bound.

As they left the Devon coast, Mendax had seen several men on horseback who had been observing the small boat. They were not native to this island and were heavily armed. These were men of the Kelanti.

CHAPTER 22

Agrar had told his people the tale of his and Agrin's experience in the Forest of the Oaks and now both Greeks and Cornish listened to Pyris and the Dog Warrior as they told of the story about Crentarus and his Demon God creating a whirlwind from hell and also of how Pyris had seen a vision of the Greek Queen Verona whose body lay in a cairn on Bodmin Moor together with the golden cup of which Pyris had no knowledge.

The Greek audience were convinced it was the hand of one of their Gods which had stopped Crentarus, whilst the Cornish who heard the story told by the Dog Warrior thought it was the intervention of their ancestor spirits and Gods who had stopped the Tantarian spy.

Agrar, Alvaria & Agrin sat together listening to all which had happened and as they did so, Agrin's imagination took over and his mind conjured up a hundred different ways in which he and his best friend Stick would have stopped and defeated Crentarus.

At this moment, Agrin started to wonder about his friend and how Mendax and he were doing on their journey east.

At the end of the storytelling, Pyris and the Dog Warrior stood facing one another, they looked deeply into one another's eyes and embraced as one would do to an old friend not seen for many a year.

The Greek and Cornish audience clapped and stamped their feet and a few moments later all the men were shaking hands with each other in acceptance of brothership on this day. Food and drink were provided for all assembled at the village.

Earlier in the morning, two more ships had left for Greece loaded with tin. The Greeks were becoming fewer and fewer in number and in a few more days, all would be gone.

As Agrar sat amongst his fellow countrymen with his family at his side, his attention was drawn way up into the afternoon sky where a bird circled above the village – this was no ordinary bird, but the giant Cornish eagle which had once more appeared in the sky, making Agrar wonder why.

The bird circled above the village for several minutes and as it did so, Agrar, Agrin, Pyris and the Dog Warrior remembered being guided by such a bird to each of their quests only days before. *Could this be the same bird?* thought each man.

The eagle started to descend and flew downwards towards a totem pole which stood in the centre of the village.

Everyone stood back as it came to land upon it. The eagle perched on the totem pole which was engraved with the names of tribal ancestors. It stood as still as night, its eyes transfixed upon Agrar and his people, its presence one of majestic appearance to all those around it.

"Do not fear this bird," said Agrar, "for it has helped us before and I think it has come once more to guide us. Be ready, fellow Agrarians, and trust in its actions."

The giant eagle outstretched its wings and squawked as loud as thunder before launching itself into the air in flight, each feather working together in harmony to give the bird lift from terra firma and defy the forces of gravity. It flew in a giant circle above the village before flying out towards the sea.

Agrin looked at his father and asked, "Father, what now?"

"Now, my son, we must all follow the giant bird as I think this is what it wishes us to do."

Moments later, the whole village together with their Greek guests charged excitedly down towards the beach where they looked out to sea at the shadow of the bird which now danced upon the Cornish waves.

Once down upon the sand, some of those assembled walked down to where the sea gently lapped against the wet sand. Others walked along the loading jetty and waited.

Pyris explained to the Greeks how the bird had guided him on Bodmin Moor and as he did this, so Agrar was telling his people his experience of seeing the eagle on his and Agrin's quest to the Forest of Oaks to restore the boy's sight.

All watched the bird's shadow, which after a while became smaller and smaller as the eagle flew higher and higher into the sky.

Agrar knew in his heart that this was a sign and that patience must prevail so he stood next to his son Agrin and said, "Let us just wait together, my son."

"Wait for what, Father?"

"Whatever the giant bird wants us to wait for."

The eagle slowly disappeared out of sight. It looked like a tiny dot as it soared high above them all.

Half an hour had passed and people slowly started to disperse. They looked at Agrar before leaving the beach to which the chieftain just smiled and nodded his head in approval of their wish to leave.

Another half an hour passed and by now, few remained waiting.

Agrar and Agrin were walking along together at the water's edge. "Father, maybe this time the eagle was mistaken, or perhaps we have misunderstood its message to us."

"Maybe so, my son, but I think a bird like that, rarely seen by man, would not act in the way it did unless it was sure of its actions."

"Will we wait much longer?" asked Agrin.

"Just for a while, my son, just for a while."

***

Agrin had an idea to take their mind away from the boredom of waiting. "I know, Father, teach me some of the fighting moves you said you would."

"Have you been practising your posture and breathing, my son?"

"Yes, Father, I have." And with that, Agrin demonstrated to his father what he had learnt and remembered from their first lesson.

"Very good, Agrin, I am proud that you listened and absorbed the knowledge I taught you."

Just as father and son were about to go through some of the basic fighting techniques and stances, a shout came from the end of the loading jetty. One of the villagers stood at the very end of it pointing out to sea at a small boat in the distance.

"What is it, Father?"

"A boat, I think, my son." Together with a small group of Greeks and villagers, they all gathered together to await and welcome the boat and its as yet unknown occupants.

The tide was going out as the craft slowly make its way in to land.

Agrin could see someone on board waving frantically at him and, within a few minutes, could make out who it was.

"It's Stick, Father."

"Are you sure, my son?"

"Oh yes, and Mendax; they have both returned, Father but why? And by boat, which is strange?"

Agrar thought the same as he and a few others waded into the sea in preparation to pull the boat up upon the sand. In it came, closer and closer, until the men grabbed a hold and pulled it as far onto the sand as they could. An excited Stick jumped out of the boat first and went over to Agrin as his father helped Mendax ashore.

"Why have you both returned?" he asked curiously.

"Agrar, Chieftain of the Agrarian people, we must go quickly and hold counsel with all from the village and surrounding area."

"But why is that so, Mendax?"

"Men of evil intention are gathering as we speak and will come in their hundreds or even thousands to kill and torture the Cornish and take your tin and wealth."

"But why?" asked Agrar.

"A new race of invaders and mercenaries called the Kelanti have control of the south of this island. They have also taken over from the sacred spiritual capital of our land and have killed the Men of the Stone Circle."

"Come, my friend, quickly to the village."

Agrar called over to Agrin and Stick to follow him and told them both sternly not to wander off but to stay close to him.

The two boatmen were also taken to the village as guests and would be fed and given a place to sleep before returning in their boat the following morning, to the settlement on the South Devon coast where they lived.

**

As Agrar's people had been robbed by visitors from afar before, the Agrarians had made beacons which had been maintained over the years in readiness for an emergency such as this. These beacons stretched along the coastline for 30 miles in each direction and also fanned out inland to other villages, settlements and tin trading communities.

Agrar gave the order for the beacons to be lit just after dusk where they would burn and warn the Cornish Bronze Age people of danger.

As Mendax sat amongst the villagers, their faces changed from one of peaceful, contented men and women to one of fear and awe. Most had never even heard of an army or a mercenary and the thought of men trained just to kill, soon coming from afar to destroy their lives and everything they lived for, was beyond their comprehension.

"What shall we do, Agrar?" shouted the men and women of the village.

Agrar and the village had just traded much tin to the Greeks who had given them many valuable things in return, making the village a prime target for the men of greed.

People started to squabble and panic at all they had heard, so Agrar stood amongst them and blew his horn. Everyone went silent and waited for the chieftain to speak.

"People of Cornwall, do not fret, but think of ways to prepare in advance before the arrival of our unwanted visitors."

"But how, Agrar?" shouted one man.

"Firstly, we have time to prepare – to hide our wealth and valuables. Secondly, pray in your hearts to the Gods and ancestors of our people, for today you all witnessed the giant eagle and how it came as a sign of the return of Mendax and Stick to us. This must mean there are things beyond our world which are helping us and lastly, remember that I and my son were guided in the oak forest and that Pyris was helped by the Gods as he tracked Crentarus."

As he spoke, the people felt reassured by his words and a great feeling and bond was felt stronger than it ever had been before by the Cornish.

Through the night, the beacons burned bright, sending the message to all fellow men and women of Cornwall. The air was alive with the sound of horns being blown to accompany the beacons in their warning.

No one knew exactly when the Kelanti would arrive, but Agrar and his people would be ready and he believed in his heart that the Gods would help them against the cruel army of men led by Vorgus.

The Kelanti had sent out fifty advanced scouting parties, each consisting of three men on horseback who would go and search out areas of potential wealth for the Kelanti army to plunder.

CHAPTER 23

A new day dawned and Agrar's people awoke with an intense fear in each of their hearts. The Agrarians had men who could fight, but not against an army of desperate and evil men. There would be the occasional local dispute over this and that but up until now the people of the Bronze Age had lived in relative peace throughout south west Britain.

Agrar had dreamt much in the night and was reminded in one of the dreams of the two mysterious spears that he and Agrin had found in the Forest of Oaks after their sight had been restored.

He decided to travel inland one mile with his son, taking the two spears with them. He did not tell of his true intentions and told people he was going to teach Agrin some hunting skills in a nearby wood.

Father and son headed away from the village and faded into the distance without raising any curiosity or suspicion from anyone. They followed a track for about twenty minutes and then broke away from it into open land.

"Father, why have we come here alone?" asked Agrin.

"My son, do not ask me why, but I believe these spears are no ordinary ones but have a power which we must now discover for ourselves."

"Oh, I see, Father."

"We must, now, this day, try to discover this power... or maybe they are no more than the type of spears we are used to."

As Agrar and Agrin were thinking of how to test the spears, Agrar's eye caught movement in the distance.

"Quick, my son, lie down and wait until I say."

They both dropped to the ground in an instant, laying side by side with spears ready in hand.

"What is it, Father?"

"Men on horseback," whispered Agrar.

The wild grass and flowers grew tall enough to hide them both and after a few minutes, Agrar raised up off the ground into a kneeling position and looked around.

Three Kelanti on horseback rode by, following the edge of the nearby wood. They carried on towards the village which immediately gave Agrar great concern.

Once it was safe to do so, both father and son doubled back to the way they had come in the hope they would see what the men were doing.

These men came with weapons, not of defence but ones of conquest and they dressed in a way never seen in Cornwall before.

Agrar was very cautious as he feared not for his own life but for his son's, who accompanied him alone.

The men disappeared out of view as Agrar and Agrin tried to follow them.

The Kelanti had made their way to a vantage point overlooking the village. Here they would spy and take note of anything that interested them. The three Kelanti scouts looked at one another with fire in their eyes. They knew there were rich pickings to be taken from Agrar's village and as they sat upon their horses they noticed the remaining Greek ships moored in the bay. Only one thing went through their minds and that was to ride back to the army of thousands of foot soldiers entering Cornwall this day. This was a prize not to be missed.

The Kelanti said few words to one another and in a short while turned their horses around to leave and return to Vorgus and his army of mercenaries.

They galloped away and were heading straight towards Agrar and Agrin. It did not take them long to see father and son, to which they drew their swords ready to charge and attack the two of them.

The sight of the three men upon horseback charging towards them made Agrar act instantly and without thinking he launched his spear at the rider to the right. The spear felt so light to the touch that Agrar thought it would lack power as it was thrown. He had worked out a trajectory of flight for the spear which it followed without deviation. The three horses were being driven hard as the horseman to the right came into contact with Agrar's gift. Although light in weight, the shiny new spearhead tore into the rider's chest and on contact it ripped into the rider's heart and shredded it to a thousand pieces. The spear travelled straight through the rider and fell to earth with its point buried in the ground and its shaft pointing skywards.

The other two Kelanti watched in horror at this and deviated away from Agrar and Agrin, giving them both a wide berth.

Now Agrin instinctively held his spear as the riders passed them at speed.

"Quick, my son, throw your spear or they will be out of range."

Agrin hesitated, much to his father's annoyance, but when it seemed the riders were out of range he threw his spear with all his might.

"It's too late, Agrin!" shouted his father but instead of gravity affecting the flight of the spear, pulling it gradually down to earth, it just kept flying through the air and seemed to travel on its own.

The riders did not see Agrin launch his spear and within a few seconds it had struck into the back of one of them. Again, the spear tore into his body and straight through it as it shredded anything it came into contact with.

The remaining rider stopped and looked back at both Agrar and Agrin. They had both used their spears and were now defenceless, so he decided to charge at them both with the intention of killing them and avenging his fellow Kelantis' deaths, which their spears had brought about.

"Stand behind me, Agrin," said Agrar as they were both charged by a screaming and angry Kelanti mercenary whose horse was coming towards them at a very fast pace.

Agrar was once again worried, not for himself, but for his son. His plan was to try and grab the rider's leg or clothing and pull him off his horse.

Closer and closer charged the horse with the rider's right arm outstretched with sword in hand.

Agrar could beat any man in a fight on sand or soil but the Kelanti had a distinct advantage on horseback as he rode straight at him with rage now flowing in every part of his mind and body.

Closer and closer the horse galloped until it was right in front of Agrar who, as it came within a few feet, leapt to one side, trying to grab the leg of the rider. The precise timing for this was slightly out and the Kelanti sword made contact with Agrar's right forearm, cutting into it as the horse and rider passed him. Agrar fell to the floor and as he did so, Agrin rushed over to him in a state of bewilderment.

"Father, are you all right?"

"My arm is cut badly, my son."

"What can I do, Father?"

"When he charges at me again you must run and hide over there in that wood."

"But I cannot leave you, Father."

"But you must, my son, or you will die with me."

"Then that is what I shall do, for it is my choice as your son."

The Kelanti horseman readied himself in preparation to charge at Agrar and Agrin once more.

Father and son had no weapons to defend themselves and Agrar was losing much blood from his wound.

Agrin stood up and in a loud and powerful voice he shouted up into the sky above, "O, Gods and ancestors of our people, I call upon you to save us from this fate. We, the Agrarians of Cornwall, need your protection now from the invaders who have come across the sea and show no respect to you or this land."

The Kelanti mercenary laughed at this and shouted mockingly, "You shall now join your so-called Gods and ancestors in the afterlife and soon we shall take this land for ourselves and kill your families and your people."

***

Agrar's heart sank as he sat holding his badly cut arm, trying to stop it bleeding.

Agrin stood in defiance of the lone Kelanti mercenary who was now ready to take their lives and then return to Vorgus and report the huge wealth in the area from tin trading.

Agrar's village would become the main target for the Kelanti to plunder.

The mercenary raised his arm with sword in hand, ready to cut down Agrin and was only moments away from charging at the boy and his father when suddenly a screech came from high above him. It was the giant Cornish eagle diving down upon him with its large powerful talons ready to teach the foreign invader a lesson.

The Kelanti mercenary could not work out what was happening and within seconds, the mighty eagle's talons latched onto his face as its beak started to tear off his nose. The screams of terror and agony rang out into the air; neither Agrar or his son had ever heard such unearthly sounds of pain before.

Agrar stood up next to Agrin and both turned their heads away from the butchery happening in front of them.

The Kelanti fell from his horse as the eagle finally let go of his head, his face torn to pieces. He was still alive but had no nose, eyes or tongue.

The eagle flew up into the sky as Agrar and his son started to walk back to the village.

"Come, my son, we can do nothing for him," said Agrar, who had almost stopped the bleeding from his arm.

They followed the track back to the village and soon had it in their sight. Just as this happened they both heard the eagle screech once more. They looked up at it and noticed its talons carrying something.

"What now, Father?" asked Agrin.

"I do not know, my son, but your prayers were answered this day and the eagle saved us from death."

The eagle opened its talons and two objects fell to earth landing a little way in front of them.

"Father, the bird has returned our spears which we had forgotten about."

"Yes, Agrin, that is so and we are truly blessed by the Gods this day."

Father and son returned to the village, safe in the knowledge that the army of Kelanti would not come so quickly to them now that the three scouts could not report back to Vorgus, but they would come soon and then Agrar and his people would face total extermination.

The giant eagle flew away to whence it came and was never seen or heard of again.

CHAPTER 24

During the next few days, Agrar rested and gave his wound time to start healing.

Mendax attended to him, bringing fresh herbs and medicines made by him.

Everyone had been told of the deaths of the three Kelanti scouts and the whole of western Cornwall got ready as best they could for the imminent and forthcoming invasion.

Two weeks passed and the last Greek ship was loaded with tin and ready to leave, taking Pyris home to Caspitaria.

Agrar had now recovered from his injury and stood on the loading jetty together with Agrin, Stick, Mendax, Alvaria and the Dog Warrior who had all come to say goodbye to Pyris, whom they had all become very fond of. Agrar presented the Greek with a gold wrist torque engraved with the pattern of the Agrarian tribe.

Pyris received this gift most graciously and returned gifts of his own sword to Agrar, his battle helmet to Agrin and jewellery to Alvaria. A deep bond, never to be broken, now existed between them all and between all the Greeks who had previously sailed homewards.

The Greek Gods had helped Pyris in his mission as did the Cornish and their Gods.

There was total silence as the Greek ship gently slipped away and out to sea. It was July 9th 1000BC, the era of the late Bronze Age where three metals were now used. Bronze, an alloy of copper and tin found here in Cornwall and gold found in abundance on Britain's sister island which would one day be named Ireland.

Into the distance sailed Pyris and his men aboard a ship which would have to travel nearly six thousand miles home. How were the rest of the fleet fairing as they sailed home? Had any ships been lost due to the weather, attacked by pirates or their bitter enemy the Tantarians?

***

As the days passed and life returned to normal, people began to relax and forget about the Kelanti as they thought their village and community was too far to the west for them to bother with. Agrar and Agrin had killed the Kelanti scouts, so how could Vorgus know of the wealthy village and surrounding area where many men of tin lived and worked with this metal?

What Agrar did not know was that one of the horses had made its way back to where the Kelanti were massing. The horse was immediately taken to Vorgus who knew about combat and horses. It did not take him long to work out his men had been attacked, especially as this horse was covered in the blood of one of his mercenaries. The Kelanti knew where this horse and its rider had been sent and were now nearing Agrar's village to take revenge upon them as well as the normal atrocities committed by the Kelanti.

***

Agrar and Agrin had gone down to the beach to practice some new fighting techniques.

It would take time to learn how to fight upon the sand but Agrin was most determined to achieve this skill with the help of his father who was now fully recovered from his sword injury and bore a large scar across the upper part of his right arm.

Father and son carried with them at all times the spears which Cassitar had left them both to help defend the Cornish, both spears having incredible power which could only be harnessed and used by the hands of Agrar and Agrin. Whilst they both practised upon the sand, Stick came running on to the beach frantically waving his hands into the air. Agrar's attention was drawn to this, but not Agrin's as his concentration in learning to fight had blinkered out all distractions.

"Agrin, Stick is here," said Agrar.

This caught Agrin's attention, "Stick, Stick, over here," he shouted out to his friend.

There was a look in fear in Stick's face and eyes as he approached them both.

"What is wrong?" asked both father and son.

Stick gasped for breath as he had run as fast as he could from the village.

"Kelanti, Kelanti!" he shouted.

"Kelanti, here, are you sure, Stick?" asked Agrar.

Stick waited awhile to catch his breath and then continued to say, "The village is surrounded by an army of thousands of men."

Agrar was not expecting this and looked directly at his son, the two of them instinctively gathered their spears and were about to leave the beach when a group of men on horseback rode onto the sand and headed in a slow but menacing way towards the three Agrarians.

Agrar and Agrin's grips tightened around the spears as Stick stood slightly behind them, feeling very vulnerable as he could not fight and had no weapon.

The horses drew nearer and the faces of the riders were clearly visible, these were hard and battle ready faces, ready to take another's life without conscience or remorse.

Agrar had seen a few men like this in his lifetime but the boys had not, which scared them both.

A large man dismounted and walked towards them. Agrar stepped a few paces forward, instructing the two boys to stay put. "Who are you?" asked Agrar.

"I am Vorgus, leader of the Kelanti," came the reply.

He was stocky and with very broad shoulders, his upper body strength was incredible and he loved to show off his muscles when he could. His hair was thick, almost like strands of rope which hung from his head to his shoulders. Unshaven and with granite-like facial features, he was most intimidating in every way possible.

"Are you from the village of tin?" he asked.

"Yes, I am Agrar, chieftain and leader to the Agrarian people of this island."

Vorgus laughed and tried to taunt Agrar by saying, "So you are Agrar, who plays with children upon the sand, you surely are a mighty chieftain."

The men on horseback behind him all laughed as did Vorgus.

"I am teaching my son to fight."

"To fight, Agrar, but why here?"

"So that my son can master the art of fighting upon sand."

The Kelanti laughed once again at Agrar and the two boys.

Vorgus walked around Agrar and then went over to Stick and Agrin, "Do you want to grow up like your father?" he asked.

"Yes, I do."

"Then I have some good news for you boy, because we will take you and train you in the way of the Kelanti."

"My father will stop you doing that!"

"No, you are wrong, boy, because soon your father will be dead, or my slave."

Agrar decided to say something as both boys were becoming very scared.

"Stop, Vorgus, why do you strike fear into the hearts of children?"

"Because they need to know and fear me and the Kelanti, who will in a very short while descend upon your village and take what they want.

Agrar knew this would involve murder and rape as well as torture, humiliation and slavery.

"No!" shouted Agrar. "I will not let it happen to my family and my people."

More laughter came from the Kelanti as more men on horseback arrived. The Kelanti army of men on foot had started to close in on the village where every man, woman and child waited with weapons of bronze made with the tin of Cassitar, all ready to fight and die defending their village and way of life.

Vorgus looked at the spears which Agrar and Agrin held in their hands. "What sort of spears do you call those, mighty Chieftain?"

For some reason, Agrin responded by shouting out, "These spears will stop you and your army from taking our land and were a gift from the God of the Agrarian race."

"No man or God has ever stopped the Kelanti before or ever will," sneered Vorgus.

Vorgus looked at Stick and asked him who he was.

"Me, I'm just a boy from the village, watching my best friend how to fight."

Vorgus had never seen such an odd looking boy before and as he continued to look at him, his curiosity increased. "Are you a native here, boy?"

"No, I was brought here as a baby and abandoned, but now I am an Agrarian and Agrin's mother and father are my family."

"What is your name, boy?"

"Stick."

"What sort of name is that?"

"Leave the boy alone, Vorgus, can't you see he is scared?" said Agrar.

"Are you scared, boy?" asked Vorgus.

Stick decided to speak up for himself as he realised the Kelanti would do whatever they liked to them anyway. He also felt that somehow his life was about to change.

"Are you scared, boy?" repeated Vorgus.

Stick went and stood directly in front of him and looked up at what was a giant compared to him. "Yes, I am scared but not of you but for you."

Vorgus and the Kelanti riders burst out laughing.

"Why and how is that so?" said Vorgus.

"Because Agrar can beat any man including you in a fight or in warfare."

"Is this so, Agrar?" asked Vorgus.

Agrar had a plan in his mind and felt he must go with his instincts as it seemed the only way out for him and his people. He looked Vorgus straight in the eye and challenged him in combat by saying, "Fight me on the sand and if I win, go and leave my people in peace."

"And if you lose, Agrar?"

"Then you shall do what you came here to do in the first place but promise me you will spare these two boys and also my wife."

"I will spare them, Agrar and teach them the ways of the Kelanti. The boys will be made slaves and sold if they do not follow our ways."

"What will become of my wife?" asked Agrar.

"If you lose the fight she will become my bed companion at night and I shall have you staked out on the ground for a few days before you die, that way you can listen to your wife's cries of pleasure as I take her each night."

Agrar passed his spear to Stick and as he raised his arm to take the weapon, Vorgus noticed the tattoo of a raven beneath the boy's armpit and recognised it and its significance.

CHAPTER 25

For over a thousand years, the people known as the Salbs had been the patriarchs of Stonehenge before being killed by the Kelanti. The ruling family of the Salbs were treated like kings and queens over them and were now all dead... or were they?

The last male child born to the ruling family was rejected by them and taken far to the west where he was abandoned. All babies born to these rulers were tattooed at one month old with the image of a raven beneath the left armpit.

Stick had such a tattoo, which Vorgus had recognised but did not comment upon.

At the age of six months, it was decided by the Salbs to either abandon or sacrifice Stick to the Gods. Even as a newborn he looked rather odd and had terrible trouble at feeding times. Stick's mother objected to him being taken away but his father and the male dominated elders made sure he was taken far away where he was eventually found at Agrar's village.

An old lady had looked after the baby upon taking pity upon it, but she had died when Stick was only seven, leaving him to fend for himself, as most people thought him cursed due to his strange appearance.

However, at this present time and unbeknownst to him, Stick was the only surviving member of the patriarch rulers of Stonehenge.

Mendax also knew of Stick's true identity as this had been revealed to him in recent dreams.

***

Kelanti mercenaries lined the clifftops and beach-head, looking down upon the beach, waiting for Vorgus to attack the village now surrounded by several thousand of his men. Vorgus had promised them great riches which he had always done, this made the men bloodthirsty and ready to kill indiscriminately.

Agrar and Vorgus stood out on the sand ready to fight for their honour. The two boys stood watching to one side, each holding tight to the magical and deadly spears within their hands.

Vorgus adopted a fighting stance whilst Agrar stood impassively upright, legs slightly apart and bent. He knew the sand well and had trained even the muscles in his feet and on his soles to work for him in a fight.

Vorgus edged closer to the chieftain grunting heavily as he did so whilst Agrar just stood and put his hands upon his hips in a rather defiant manner. He was baiting Vorgus to lash out at him and make the first strike.

The two men were within the striking range of a punch and the impatient Kelanti leader let out a big grunt as he lunged forward with a right punch aimed at Agrar's head, whose response to this was to step back with his left leg, turning his hips clockwise, using this rotation to generate power into his right arm which would now retaliate against Vorgus.

As Agrar stepped back out of range from the attacking fist, he too formed a fist with the middle knuckle sticking out further than the other fingers. This was a specialist strike and as Vorgus' right arm stretched out in an attempt to punch him, Agrar struck hard and with deadly accuracy onto the radial nerve running along Vorgus' inner right forearm. This resulted in extreme pain for him and created a dead arm for a short while.

"You move like the wind, Agrarian," commented Vorgus, to which Agrar said nothing in return.

Agrar was totally detached from thought as the two men began their combat. If he had reacted to the terrible things Vorgus had said then Agrar's emotions may have interfered with his ability to fight, using his brain and not his body in a state of rage which was now happening to Vorgus.

Every time the Kelanti leader struck out at Agrar he would either block, dodge or strike the attacking weapon. Vorgus was a large man and soon started to tire as the sand added extra effort for him to contend with. He decided to remove all his clothes in an attempt to confuse and undermine Agrar. His muscles were of more than normal proportion and definition as he stood totally naked in front of Agrar, trying again to taunt him by saying, "Look at me, Agrar, and look at my body which will soon be on top of your wife each night to pleasure her."

This attempt at provoking Agrar nearly worked, especially as it was witnessed by the two boys, Agrin and Stick, who were standing just yards away. He had no choice but to teach Vorgus a lesson without taking his life, as he feared the Kelanti would go on the rampage in retaliation. He pretended to rant and rave in anger at what had just been said to him about his wife.

Vorgus thought the chieftain had lost his temper which would affect the effectiveness of his fighting skills, so charged at Agrar like a wild bull, his head low and arms outstretched in the hope of achieving a frontal bear hug.

Agrar immediately anticipated this and raised his left arm high into the air.

As the two men came together Vorgus wrapped his arms around Agrar ready to put on the bear hug and take him to the ground.

At precisely the right moment as the lock went on and their bodies started to drop to the sand, Agrar's left arm came crashing down with the tip of his elbow striking into the back of Vorgus' head resulting in him being instantly knocked clean out.

Agrar walked over to the boys as some of the Kelanti rode over and dismounted from their horses to give aid to their unconscious leader, who in a short while regained consciousness.

Vorgus was not pleased and quickly dressed, he whispered into the ear of one of his men who got on his horse and rode off with two other Kelanti mercenaries. He walked over to Agrar and the boys and said, "Well, Agrar, you have shown me you can trick and beat me upon the sand and for this you gain my respect."

"Then if you truly respect me, go now and leave this place and my people in peace."

"If that were only possible, mighty Chieftain."

"You said that if I beat you in combat you would do this."

"Yes, I did that, but my men did not fight you and they number in their thousands, they need your wealth for themselves."

Agrar had already thought about this sort of treachery and knew the Kelanti would do as they wanted so he now decided to insult Vorgus.

"May the God of my people smite you and your men down."

Vorgus laughed loudly and replied, "You Agrarians have no God, so do not waste your time in trying to invoke him as I have already sent my men to order the attack on your village."

Agrar took hold of his spear from Stick and dropped to his knees whilst holding it. He shut his eyes and recalled when he had no sight in the Forest of Oaks. As he did this, his whole body tingled and his spear became warm to the touch with its bronze tip glistening in the sunlight.

Vorgus laughed once more and then mounted his horse and rode off with the remaining men to help in the attack on Agrar's village.

"What shall we do, Father?" shouted Agrin.

"Kneel next to me, my son and hold your spear with your eyes closed and remember back to what happened to us both in the Forest of Oaks where we were both blind."

As Agrar and his son did this, watched by a rather nervous Stick, the Kelanti army descended upon the village, an army of over three thousand in number against less than two hundred Agrarians defending their way of life.

As Agrar and Agrin remembered back to the Forest of Oaks, their spear tips sent back into the sky, rays of sparkling light which lit up the heavens even though it was daytime.

***

The Cornish Tin God Cassitar took breath and in his belly lay his metal in molten form. He released his breath upon the land of Cornwall and a hundred thousand globules of liquid tin were sent raining down upon the land. Each globule solidified and shaped itself into a razor sharp arrowhead of tin. No shaft or feathers were needed to help propel Cassitar's gift to the Kelanti who were only yards from the Cornish men, women and children defending Agrar's village.

The sky went from one of incredible white light to one of total darkness as the tin arrowheads honed in on their intended Kelanti victims who suddenly stopped and looked skywards as Cassitar's gifts to them whistled through the air on their flight.

The people of Cornwall were safe from Cassitar's deadly weapon as they all had traces of tin in their blood and could not be harmed by the arrow tips.

Agrar and the two boys could hear the noise from the beach and started to make their way back to the village, they knew their prayers had been answered.

Each Kelanti mercenary was struck many times by the tin arrowheads which, once they had penetrated the body, would spin fiercely inside their victims, destroying their vital organs.

In just a few moments, the whole army of over three thousand men lay dead – that is, except for one man who stared out in bewilderment at his army of corpses. It was Vorgus, who for some reason had been spared from death.

The Cornish men and women could not believe what had just happened and knew in their hearts that this was not the work of a mortal man.

As Agrar and the boys reached the village, Alvaria ran out to them and embraced each in turn.

By now, an angry mob surrounded Vorgus, the sole survivor – they were intent on killing him.

Agrar blew his horn and made his way through the crowd standing next to the Kelanti leader who was still mounted upon his horse.

"Go now!" shouted Agrar. "Go now to whence you came from, to the land of your fathers, across the sea, never to return to this island or to Cornwall again."

Vorgus nodded in a defeated manner.

"Tell of this day and warn others whose wish to come here, that we the Agrarians are protected by the God of Tin who looks over us and will kill any army which comes here to conquer us."

The crowd stood back as Vorgus' horse gently trotted out and away from the village.

***

Cassitar's ancient people of Bronze Age Cornwall were safe and would always have his protection as long as his tin would be used to make bronze, the metal of the Gods.

Buzzards and birds of prey feasted for many days upon the bodies of the fallen Kelanti army and at night, wolves, foxes and wild dogs did the same.

Vorgus was never seen or heard from again and did indeed return to the mainland of northern Europe where he lived in solitude, his spirit broken by the annihilation of his army.

***

All the Greek ships returned safely to Caspitaria where the Cornish tin which had travelled almost six thousand miles, was melted down and mixed with copper. The bronze created by this ancient metallurgy easily matched that of Pyris' enemies, the Tantarians.

Both Pyris and Aquilla fought alongside one another in the many battles which took place, until eventually the Tantarians were defeated by such men and by the special bronze used in their weaponry, which contained the power and magic of Cassitar's Cornish tin.

***

EPILOGUE

In 1837, looters raided a Bronze Age burial cairn at Rillaton upon Bodmin Moor.

Inside, they discovered a beautiful golden cup. Was this the cup protecting Cornwall's wealth and prosperity?

In the story of Agrar of the Cornish, Queen Verona was buried in such a cairn at Rillaton.

Could this be the same golden cup which was buried with her?

The legend told that Queen Verona would one day be reincarnated and rule a mighty empire, so was it coincidence that in the same year of 1837 when the gold cup was discovered, a new queen would come to the throne and rule Britain? Her name was Victoria. Was she the reincarnation of Verona?

Both of their names start and finish with the same letter.

***

The tin industry in Cornwall slowly started to decline from around this time.

Was this in any way connected with the cup's discovery?

Queen Verona was Greek and just over one hundred years later in 1947, Queen Victoria's great granddaughter Elizabeth married a Greek Prince.

Was there a connection here or was it just another unexplainable coincidence between Greece and the island of Britain?

***

The next time you are in London you can see the golden cup found on Bodmin Moor in 1837. It is known as the Rillaton Cup and is housed at the British Museum, London, England. Look upon it and feel its splendour and magnificence, for it is a reflection of wealth and life during the Bronze Age where two metals ruled the world.

Much of Cassitar's tin still lies waiting beneath the ground, ready for the time when man shall once again need and use it. No one knows when this will happen but it will come one day as it is the destiny of Cornwall, just as Cassitar intended it to be.

***

The spirit of Agrar and his people still live on to this day, engrained into the people known as the Cornish, whose blood still flows with the memory of the ancient ones of tin within it.

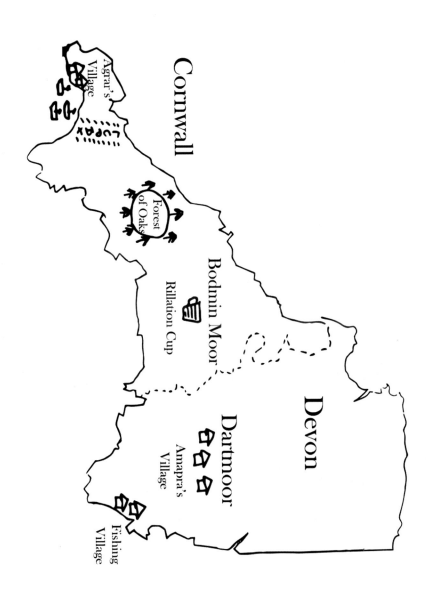

Cornwall

Agrar's Village

LUPAX

Forest of Oaks

Bodmin Moor

Rillation Cup

Devon

Dartmoor

Amapra's Village

Fishing Village

The following photos are of some of the amazing Bronze Age metal detecting finds made by the author. These finds do not form any part of a hoard but were found individually by him over an 8-year period. Also pictured are some of the 400 Neolithic/early Bronze Age worked flints he has found lying on the surface of fields whilst field walking.

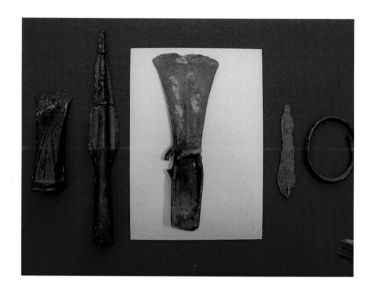